Captive Assassins

Mackenzie Ostrowski

ISBN: 9781079828337

Dear Reader,

Before you read this, I'd like you to know that what I'm about to say is important to this storyline. My name is Mackenzie Ostrowski. I wrote this novel when I was only twelve and had it published a few months after my thirteenth birthday. I had so many people tell me I was too young to accomplish something this big, but the truth is, age should never define one's limits. Writing this story has been quite the adventure, and I plan on writing many more. This book isn't dedicated to anyone, and it has no hidden meaning. I was genuinely looking for something to occupy me and ended up falling in love with it. Thank you for choosing this book, I hope you enjoy.

CONTENTS

i

ACKNOWLEDGMENTS

I have so many things to say, but I'd like to begin by thanking the reader again for choosing this book. I genuinely appreciate the time you've put into simply deciding to read this story, and I truly hope you enjoy it. I'd also like to thank my parents for all of the effort that they have put into helping me through the publishing process. I'd like to thank my editor especially for all of the hard work and time she put into this. I'm beyond grateful for all of the constructive criticism I've received. I'd also like to thank my siblings and friends for the interest they've shown, and the encouragement and motivation they've given me, especially in times I felt like giving up. This has been such an amazing experience for me, and it couldn't have been possible without you all. *Captive Assassins* is the first book of a trilogy that I hope to complete within the next two years. Afterwards, I have many stories that I plan on writing as well as some inspirational works, and books that I hope will raise awareness about the world around us. I hope that I will be able to influence and inspire all of the wonderful people around me. No matter our age, gender, or race, we all have a story inside of us. I hope that we will all continue to pursue them

I

New York City is very busy, but the traffic isn't what kept me awake last night. I spent the last eight hours lying in my bed, counting the passing seconds. I'm sure my clock was ticking way too slow, but it doesn't matter. Time is the last thing on my mind right now. My alarm was screaming at me by the time the wind from last night's storm finally stopped. The label gave me a reminder for my grandpa's funeral today. I didn't want to get up.

I slipped out of bed and put on a lacy black dress and hat. As I got ready, I reminded myself once again that I'm going to be okay. My name is Rohana Walters, by the way. Everyone calls me Rose. I have long, reddish-brown hair and pale blue eyes, and the fairest skin you will ever see. My friends all think I'm absolutely gorgeous, but I know they are just saying that to be nice. Most people do, anyway. The truth is, I've never really had a problem with my appearance. After about half an hour of working with my hair, makeup, and outfit, I finally gave my mirror a look of satisfaction.

"Mia," I asked, "Did you remember to buy your flowers for Grandma?" Mia is my little sister. She can be a bit of a pain, but I love her more than anything. She's only ten years old, so she didn't know Grandpa like I did. She still loved him though; it just didn't hit her as hard when we heard about his heart attack.

"Oh, no! I completely forgot!"

Of course she did.

"I'll drive by the store on the way to Grandma's house, okay?"

"Okay. Thanks, Rose."

Mia is pretty smart for her age. She is a grade ahead in school and she's still at the top of her class. She just forgets things easily. She's also really small and light, but it's never held her back.

"Here, put this on," Mia offered me a long, black trench coat that hung a few inches below my maxi dress.

"It's pretty cold outside, you'll need it."

"Good idea, Mia," I forced myself to smile and pretended I didn't know that Mia saw me holding back tears. "Now get in the car, we're going to be late."

"It's okay," she opened the car door, "I miss him too. Now, do you think that Grandma will like roses or poppies? Oh! Or she may like...." I didn't pay attention to the rest. I was more occupied with my speech that I had to give today.

I ran into Flowers on First by myself to get a small bouquet and walked up to a clerk.

"Excuse me, I'm looking specifically for yellow

camellia flowers, where can I find those?"

"Right this way," he led me to the back of the shop.

"Thanks!"

"Just take some, we have a ton."

"Are you sure? I wouldn't want to be an inconvenience."

"No, it's fine. My name is Alexander, by the way,"

He looked really nice, to be honest. Tall, about my age, brown eyes and wispy brown hair. He wasn't being sympathetic. He was being kind.

"I'm Rose. Thanks for letting me have the flowers. Sorry if I sounded rude."

"You didn't. And you're welcome."

"Have a nice day."

"You too."

I left the store in a hurry, knowing I was already late for Grandma's. When I got in the car, I handed Mia the flowers and drove away quickly. It was pretty cold outside. Droopy and foggy. I couldn't help but wonder if this was the way that the world was now; if Grandpa's absence robbed the world of the happy yellow sunshine.

Grandpa died on a business trip in Paris, France. He was retired, so it wasn't exactly business, but he was there to help an informal student of his. About two weeks ago, Grandma received a call from a hospital saying that Grandpa had a heart attack and died an hour later. Grandma had so many questions, but before she could ask anything, the woman on the phone hung up. The next day, Grandma received a death certificate signed by two doctors and the man Grandpa was visiting.

Grandma contacted the hospital and they strangely refused to send in autopsy data or even send the body to New York for the funeral. Today we will be burying Grandpa's favorite belongings. Anyone who heard the story would know something was wrong. I had difficulty believing that Grandpa just died without proof and his body was in custody. And of course, I couldn't resist a good mystery, so I've been doing my own thinking.

I know it sounds awful to be entertained by the

recent death of a relative, but I promise that's not the

case. I'm truly devastated that Grandpa is gone. Not

dead, but just missing. I don't think Grandpa died. I

think he was kidnapped. He was healthy, and never

showed any signs of heart failure.

I've done so much research over the past two weeks.

The hospital that called us is real. I had my own physician

verify the death certificate, which was also real. Who says a

doctor can't be a criminal, though? I'm sure Grandpa's so-

called student was in on it, too. The woman who called us

could've been involved, too, or maybe not. Maybe I'm just

going crazy.

"Hey, Rose?" Mia spoke from the backseat.

"Yes?" I almost forgot she was even in the car.

"You missed the turn."

I missed the turn. When I get to thinking I tend to focus a little too hard.

"Sorry, Mia," I chuckled, "what would I do without you?"

"You probably would have ran that red light," she joked.

I turned around and drove up the road to Grandma's. When I arrived at the gate, I reached out the window and pressed the button on the keypad.

"Hello?" A voice came through the speaker.

"Hi, Mr. Lewis. It's Rose," David Lewis was one of the many butlers and maids who worked for my grandparents. Grandpa was a Neurosurgeon, best in the nation, and very famous. He was extremely rich, but also kind and selfless. We were never treated as if we were not good enough. I often took Mia to dinner over here and Grandma would take her to plays and dances. Grandpa and I would spend hours on the roof and stargaze. They loved spoiling us, especially Grandpa. His son, my father, refused to accept money from him though, so we never had much at home. I rarely understood my parents. They were always fighting.

"Oh, hello Rose. Come in. Your grandmother is waiting for you in the study."

The extravagant gate opened up, and I drove up the long brick driveway. Fountains and statues, long rows of carefully cut hedges, roses, sunflowers, and willow trees lined the driveway. Gardeners trimmed and watered the plants and another steward, the pastry chef I think, walked alongside my car. She knocked on the window, and I rolled it down.

"Miss Walters," She spoke hastily, "I understand that you have little time here, however, would you like me to alert the staff to prepare breakfast and tea for you?"

"Oh, no thank you. We're going out."

"Do you need a guard to accompany you?"

"That will be unnecessary, ma'am. Thank you for your concern." I rolled up my window and pulled up to the house.

"Please smooth you skirt, Mia," I helped her out of the car. We walked up to the grand front doors and Mr. Lewis came to greet us.

"Right this way." He led us up the grand staircase and into the study where Grandma was sitting. Before he shut the door he whispered, "I'm so sorry about your grandfather. It really is a shame he left us so soon."

"Grandma!" Mia ran in and gave her a hug.

"Hello, Mia," Grandma hugged her back.

"These flowers are for you," she handed her the camellia flowers that I got earlier.

"Thank you, Mia," she stood up. I thanked Lewis and walked over.

"Hi, Grandma," I kissed her cheek," How are you?"

"Better," she smiled.

I knew she was lying. Grandma wasn't better at all. She and I have the same idea about Grandpa. She was definitely worried, but she hid it well.

"Good."

"I'll tell the kitchen to set up the tea."

"Actually, I told the chef not to. I thought we could go out. There's a little place on Sixteenth Street that I think you'd like."

"It's called Whitehouse Café," Mia said, "and I love it there. Can we please go?"

"Of course! It sounds lovely."

"Alright," I said, "let's go. I hope you don't mind sitting with Mia; I've got some things in the passenger seat."

"Oh, that's fine, she makes good company." I walked back into the courtyard and helped Grandma into the car. I'm glad we decided to go out.

III

When we arrived at the café, I had a difficult time keeping my jaw off of the floor when I saw Alexander working as a barista.

"Alexander?" I was hoping that I didn't sound awkward, but even if I did, this situation gave me a good excuse.

"Who's Alexander?" typical Mia, always the first to ask.

"Oh, hi Rose! What can I get you today?" Alexander asked from behind the counter. He was acting like he hadn't been working a completely different job that morning.

"I thought you were a florist." It was supposed to be a joke, but I don't think it sounded like it.

"I was just... um... filling in for... a friend. Yeah, a friend. Just this morning."

I don't even think he was trying to be convincing.

"Okay." I said, clearly confused.

"I said, who's Alexander?" Mia demanded.

"He was the person who sold me the flowers for Grandma."

"Oh, cool. Is it okay if I just call him Alex, though? Alexander is too long."

"Mia, don't be rude."

"You can call me Alex if you want," he broke the awkward silence "That's what most people call me, anyway."

"I'll have a mocha and a blueberry muffin, please." I said quickly.

"Sounds great," he put in the order.

Mia and Grandma both ordered a chocolate muffin with steamed milk, and then I took Mia to an outdoor table. Grandma stayed inside and talked to Alex for almost ten minutes, which actually seemed quite suspicious. I didn't bother saying anything, though. After all, Grandma was an honest person.

"So, are you excited for the lantern ceremony tonight?" I asked Mia with an innocent look. The lantern ceremony was not really an official ceremony, more of a tradition. My great uncle had the idea to send a floating lantern to the relative who had passed. In the lantern you could paste or pin a message or picture.

"Yeah, I guess." She finished her muffin. "I forgot my camera, so I guess I'll have to draw a picture for Grandpa, instead of sending him a picture."

"That's fine. You are a pretty good artist."

"Something like that. So, how's work?" I could tell she was trying to change the subject.

"It's great."

I'm only seventeen. I work at a local library and pay the bills on a small apartment that my parents used to live in. I know it's technically illegal, but Mia is my responsibility now. My parents died in a car crash three years ago. It didn't feel right to live with my Grandparents after the accident, so I just decided to drop out of school and started working. My teachers didn't seem to have a problem with my decision, as I was already taking college courses. I've always been smarter than most people my age; I guess it runs in the family. Now, my independence is normal to our family.

"Did you get the promotion?"

"I don't know yet. My boss will tell me tomorrow."

"When I grow up, I want to be just like you." Mia made sure to tell me this as often as she could.

"No, you don't," I sighed. "Mia, what job do you want to have when you grow up?"

"A zookeeper, why?"

"I think you'll make an excellent zookeeper, but only if you promise me one thing."

"What's that?"

"You have to be yourself. Don't ever try and be someone else, okay?"

"Okay, but can I still be *like* you?"

"Of course."

"Good, because I want to be independent, and strong, and kind, and honest, and positive. That's exactly like you."

"You really think I'm all those things, Mia?" I almost started to cry.

"Of course I do."

"I love you, Mia."

"I love you, too."

"Now, what do you say we get to Central Park?"

IV

When we arrived at the Park, I was surprised to see the area completely packed. I honestly didn't know that so many people would be here. Grandma had reserved a small chunk of Central Park for the funeral. It was decorated with yellow roses and old-fashioned golden lights strung between the trees. The sky was still dark grey from last night's storm, so the whole thing felt quite cozy.

"Rose!" My best friend Blair, who I have known since I was two, ran up to me and gave me a huge hug.

"Blair! I'm so glad you could make it."

"You know I couldn't just leave you alone like this. Besides, I haven't seen you in forever!"

"You saw me last week."

"That's way too long, and you know it."

"You look amazing. I didn't expect you to put so much effort into a couple of hours," I shook my head. Truth is, I did expect it. Blair was the type of person to go above and beyond expectations. It was less of an expectation, and more of anticipation.

Blair and I are the same age, but that's our only physical similarity. She has beautiful dark skin and short, curly brown hair. Her deep green eyes are the most beautiful thing I've ever seen, and to top it all off, she has the most adorable freckles lining her cheeks and nose. I'm a bit taller than her, but I wouldn't consider her short.

"Are you kidding me?" she said, "you're the star of the show! You're absolutely gorgeous! But that's not what matters right now," she sighed, "are you okay?"

"Yeah, I'm doing fine."

"Is there anything I can get you?" I changed the

subject, "Coffee, or maybe a pastry?"

"No, thanks. I ate on the way here. How is your day so far?"

"Good. It's been pretty eventful so far."

"What kind of eventful?"

We moved over to a small picnic table by some trees.

"Well I met this guy at the flower shop on First."

"Go on." Blair said with amusement.

"And he sold me some flowers for Grandma, since Mia forgot them at home. Well, he actually gave them to me, but that's not the point. Before I keep going, I would like to make it clear that he was actually working there."

"Oh, really? I thought a random stranger handed

you some flowers! My bad." Blair always joked around with me.

"After I got the flowers, I went to Grandma's, and then the little café on Sixteenth Street."

"Oh, you mean that cute little muffin place?"

"Yeah! Anyway, the same guy that sold me the flowers was working as a barista."

"No." She was actually astonished this time.

"Yes, and get this, he's sitting on that bench over there right now." He really was. Alex was wearing a black hoodie and a pair of light blue jeans, sitting at a bench just outside of the closed off area for the funeral.

"You're joking. There's no way that's true unless he's following you, which is a problem."

"Yeah. I didn't think of that. I mean, I thought it

was really weird that he kept showing up, but I wasn't concerned until now. Anyway, let's just relax for a little bit. The big speeches and all start soon."

"Good idea." We talked with family and friends for the next couple of hours. Mia had told me earlier that we shouldn't be so sad about this. She said we should be celebrating Grandpa's life, and that's exactly what we were doing. There were a few tears here and there, but we were actually having a pretty good time.

It was finally time for the ceremony, and we all quieted down and took our seats. Grandma spoke first, which made all of us cry. After that, a few aunts and uncles spoke. I didn't think they even knew me, but I didn't care.

The lady before me was almost finished when I heard my name being whispered. I turned around to see Alex crouching behind the table that Blair and I were sitting at earlier.

"Rose!" He whisper-yelled. "Rose, get over here!"

"What the heck? Why on earth at you here?" I crouched and walked over to him, and thankfully, nobody noticed my absence.

"You need to get out of here." He looked genuinely concerned.

"Alex, you're starting to creep me out. Please leave." I started to walk away, but he grabbed my arm.

"No, you don't understand! *You* need to leave right now!"

"Who are you, anyway?"

"I'm a private detective hired to keep you safe. I can't explain why, and I know you don't believe me, but please. Go."

"What?"

"I can't make you leave, but you'll regret it if you don't," he said.

"Rohana Walters." Someone called from the stage. It was my turn.

"I need to go, and so do you."

I quickly made my way to the stage. No one saw me with Alex.

I walked up the stairs and began to speak. "Charles Walters-" I was cut off by a loud noise. The crowd in front of me began to scream and run frantically to their cars. Now I knew why Alex was trying to get me out of there. Now I understand why he sounded so urgent, and why he seemed so worried. Bombs.

V

They were only small explosions, I'm sure nobody was badly injured, but I could be wrong. I jumped off of the stage and ran to where Mia and Blair had been sitting. I couldn't see them though all of the frantic guests and smoke.

"Rose! Rose, where are you?" Mia was screaming for me from the trees. I ran as quickly as I could in her direction.

"Mia!" She was crouching behind a large tree stump.

"Are you okay?"

"I think so, but my eyes are burning!"

"Can you run?"

"Yeah."

"Good. Lets go!" I started sprinting to where I parked my tiny car, dodging small explosions left and right. I managed to keep Mia's hand in mine, though she ran much slower than I hoped she would.

"Wait! Blair and Grandma are still back there!" Mia yelled in between sobs. I left her near a stone fountain and soaked my smoky coat in the cold water.

"You stay here! I'm going to go back for them! Don't move! Everything is going to be all right!"

I was trying my best to be brave for her. I sprinted back to the now flaming park. Someone must have called the fire department, because there were loud sirens, caution tape, and bright yellow water hoses all over the place. I ran into the park without notice.

I was running as fast as I could, and my dress caught on a bush. It wasn't coming loose and ended up tearing badly, leaving me on the ground. My hand landed on a small flame in the grass. I immediately screamed and clutched my now terribly burned palm and fingers. I knew I didn't have much time though, so I stood up and continued running, holding back tears.

"Blair! Grandma!" I was choking on my words. Where are you?"

"Over here!" It was Blair. "Gram is hurt! She can barely walk!"

"I'm coming!" I ran over to them and draped my soaking wet coat over Grandma's shoulders. Blair and I both helped her out of the park and to the fountain. Mia was still there, crying her eyes out.

"I can drive you guys to my house." Blair panted. "My mom was going to make a stew for lunch. I don't think she'll mind the company."

"At this point, I'm too tired to argue."

I scooped Mia into my arms and carried her over to Blair's car.

"Come on, Grams. I'll help you over to my car. My mom will fix you up when we get there, okay?"

"Thank you, Blair. You really are a sweetheart."

We were all having a hard time breathing from the smoke. When we arrived at Blair's house, her mother threw the door open as soon as we rang the bell.

"Oh! Thank the heavens you're all right!" She swung her arms around us. "I saw it all on television, and I was so worried about you!" She spoke with a heavy Southern accent.

"Can they stay for lunch?" Blair coughed. Her beautiful black gown was polluted with smoke.

"Of course! Come in, come in." Blair's house was so warm and inviting. Antiques were placed on every surface you could think of. She had an old brick fireplace and a large bookshelf full of old folktales.

"Mrs. Walters!" She helped Grandma to a leather armchair. "I'll have that ankle of yours fixed up in no time. You just wait here."

"If you want to use my shower, go ahead. I have another outfit for you." Blair took me to her bathroom upstairs and handed me a clean sweater and some jeans.

"Thanks. I'll be fast. You need to rinse off, too." I quickly lathered myself in soap and washed my hair using only my right hand. My left looked awful, and the water made it sting even worse, but I knew I had to clean it. I contemplated using peroxide as a stepped out of the shower, but decided not to. I couldn't handle any more pain right now.

I put on the clothes that Blair loaned me and helped Mia get washed up, as well. Blair gave her a large t-shirt to wear as a dress. By the time we were all somewhat clean, Grandma was asleep in the same armchair with a brace on her ankle.

"Come, sit down. I've got some beef stew for y'all. It's still nice and warm." Blair's mom was always so kind. When my parents died, she offered for me to move in with them, but I refused. Sometimes I regret it.

"Thank you so much, Mrs. Davis. We really appreciate it."

I sat down next to Blair and held Mia in my lap. Once we had all finished our stew, we began to go over the day's events. I told them all about my day in detail, starting with the second I left my house. Everyone felt awful about my hand; I almost wish I hadn't mentioned it. Mrs. Davis gave me a gauze wrap for it, but it didn't do much other than stop the bleeding.

"This Alex guy seems real suspicious." Mrs. Davis sounded concerned. "I think you should call the police."

"I agree." Blair spoke up. "This is getting out of hand. I mean, what if he set up the attack?" Mia was asleep on Grandma's lap, which allowed us to be more open.

"You have a good point, but why would he tell me to leave if his goal was to get rid of me?"

"Maybe it was targeted on someone else. It could have even been Gram."

"No, it wasn't me." Grandma limped over to the table.

"Grandma, did you know about this?"

"No, I absolutely did not, believe me."

"Gram, what did you say to Alex at Whitehouse Café this morning?" Blair asked before I could.

"I simply asked what kind of flour was in my muffin. Then, I thanked him for letting me know, and on my way out, he gave me this. She handed me a small note written on the back of an old receipt.

"Triple Chocolate Muffin recipe." I read the whole thing slowly, looking for clues.

"Sounds innocent to me." Blair said with a sigh. "This whole thing seems really childish."

"Wait. Look at this. All of the letters are lowercase, except for some random ones scattered all over the place."

"I'll bet they spell out a message!" Blair took the note from my hands and grabbed a pen form a drawer in the kitchen. She started writing down the capitalized letters in order below the recipe.

"Well, what does it say?" I asked eagerly.

"Have a nice day." She replied blankly. "This is stupid."

"There went that lead." Just then, the doorbell rang. Mrs. Davis opened the door and a large man wearing glasses and a white suit pushed her aside and walked in.

"Hello, and my apologies for the intrusion." He spoke with a British accent. "My name is Mr. George Peterson, head of UIA. I'm looking for agent Rohana Walters."

VI

"I'm sorry, but I've never heard of such a person. You can leave now," Mrs. Davis began to shut the door on him, but he effortlessly stopped it with his hand.

"Well of course you have, she's sitting right over there." He held up a copy of my driver's license.

"Where did you get that?" Grandma demanded.

"I've got a copy of everyone's identification card." He took another card from his chest pocket and began to read from it. "Now, Mrs. Bella Grace Davis, would you please let me speak to Miss Walters?" He didn't wait for a response. He walked over to me, and I stood up.

"I'm not an agent. You have the wrong person."

"Well, you are correct. You're not an agent *yet*. My job is to take you to UIA's headquarters, or as you would refer to it, Europa."

"Europa?" Man hasn't even had a successful trip to Mars yet, let alone Europa. The government shut down NASA two years ago, anyway. They went bankrupt. They were losing too much money on Mars, and finally thought they could guarantee a safe trip. When it ended up failing and killing several people, they were sued and forced to shut down. Reaching Europa would be impossible. "With all due respect, Mr. Peterson, you sound crazy."

"Of course not! You're the crazy one, here. You see, UIA isn't allowed to have any contact with the less intelligent fraction of the population because they haven't unlocked the minimum percentage of the brain to understand our modern technology. Your reaction was expected, but I promise all of this is true."

"Excuse me?" Now I was just angry. "Less intelligent? Modern technology?"

"Don't worry. We will extract the memory of this conversation from your little friends here, and I'll explain the rest to you on the plane to Paris." He acted like this was no big deal.

"You can't just brainwash my family, and there's no way I'm going to Paris with some freak!" I yelled. "Besides, I thought we were talking about Europa, Paris shouldn't even have come up!"

He started to chuckle. "Of course not! You're going with me, not a freak."

He took me by the arm and started to walk towards the door. Blair ran to the door before he could reach it, locked it, and slapped Peterson across the face. He released my arm.

"She said *no*." Blair was the most angry I've ever seen her.

"Excuse me? Are you some kind of bodyguard?" Peterson was losing his temper.

"No. I'm her best friend, and the last time I checked, I don't let people take her hostage without my permission."

"You know, we could use a strong agent like you." He smirked. "How about you come with us? I won't wipe your memory, and you can train as a real bodyguard for Miss Walters. How about that?"

"Blair, please just let him take me. I don't want anything happening to you." I begged her to stay.

"Fine." She replied.

"Thank you." I was so relieved.

"No, not you, Rose," She turned back to Peterson. "I'll go on your stupid field trip, but if anything happens to her, you and your fancy little organization

37

won't see another day. You understand me?" She looked

him right in the eye.

"Fully," There was a long pause. "Now, we

wouldn't want to miss our flight. Before we leave, Miss.

Walters, I would like for you to write a small note letting

your grandmother know that you and your friend will be

leaving for a couple of weeks. We will wipe their

memories of the past six hours, and everything will go

back to normal for them. Is there anything that you would

like to pack for the trip?"

"How long will we be away?" Blair still had fire

in her eyes.

I was so confused. Could she be serious? Did she

really believe that this was real?

"Fourteen days. We have many shops on Europa,

though. You may want to consider buying our customary

apparel, as your clothes are far different from typical space fashion."

Really? Space fashion? This was the most confused I've ever been. Does he really believe we trust him?

"Did y'all forget about me?" Mrs. Davis spoke up. "If you're going to wipe my memory, then you better have my permission," even Mrs. Davis didn't seem to question it.

"Mom, you need to listen to me." Blair walked over to her. She was serious.

"I know, I know. It's for Rose. Remember though, you're going to have to take care of yourself. I won't be there for you, and we won't have contact."

"I love you, Mom," She hugged her as tight as she could. "You have to promise me to take care of them!"

"I promise." She straightened Blair's shirt. "You take lots of those selfie things for me. I got to see y'all up in space."

"I will." She turned to Peterson. "Can she please keep her memory?"

"I'm afraid not. It is against protocol, and could risk our entire organization."

"I understand, Sir." She hugged Mrs. Davis one last time. "See you in two weeks." I walked over to where I thought Grandma had fallen asleep, but she was still awake. Mia was still passed out on the couch.

"Grandma?"

"Rohana," she looked up at me with a serious expression, "You have to go. I can't explain why, but you really do need to leave. You'll be fine."

I never thought I'd doubt my own grandmother, but I did now. I've been through so much in the past few weeks, and now this. I still thought about it, and eventually made up my mind.

"Just a minute." I ran upstairs and grabbed my dress and jacket from the wash. I draped them both over Mia's fragile little body, and gave her a hug. Before we left, Peterson set a small chip on the table.

"I'm glad you agreed to accompany me," he spoke. "You made the right choice. Now, this will go off in approximately one minute. It will release an invisible gas that will make you forget all about today. Don't worry, it's completely harmless."

He rushed Blair and I out of the house and I heard a small beep coming from the chip, along with a hissing noise. The gas had been released. There was no going back.

VII

Blair and I grabbed our cell phones, jewelry, and some basic undergarments from my apartment on the way to the airport. We shared a large suitcase and stuffed some things into our handbags.

"Are you sure you want to do this?" I asked. "You know he's crazy, right? How come you're acting like this?"

"You really thought I believed him? No way! I'm calling the police."

I don't think I've ever been more relieved. I should've known better. Blair picked up her phone and started to dial 911.

"Hello," a woman on the phone spoke, "this is 911 what's your emergency?"

"Hi," Blair spoke quietly, "my name is Blair

Davis. I live downtown. I'm calling to report an attempted kidnapping. A man by the name of Peterson claims-"

"I'm sorry," the woman interrupted, "do you mean George Peterson?"

"Yes, actually, how did you-"

"Unfortunately, we will be unable to help you here. Goodbye."

The responder hung up, Blair and I were silent.

"Maybe we should just go," I sighed.

"What? Why?"

"Grandma. She told me to go. I'm choosing to trust her on this one."

"Really?"

"Yeah, she said everything would be fine. Besides, she wouldn't let us do anything that would put us in danger."

"You're right. We should go."

"You sure?"

"You know I would do anything for you, Rose. You can always count on me."

"Right back at you." I locked my front door and hid the spare key. We got in the armored white limo that was waiting for us at the door, and found Peterson waiting for us in the back. The large, buff man in the driver's seat nodded to Peterson and drove us to the airport.

"Here we are!" Peterson said enthusiastically as we pulled up to the massive building.

"What time is the flight?" I asked.

"Seven o'clock. We have plenty of time."

"That will be great for explaining to us why we're being launched into space unwillingly." I was starting to adopt Blair's attitude.

"Ah, yes. About that, I would like to apologize for being so abrupt." He definitely wasn't sorry.

"It's all right. People get kidnapped and forced into intergalactic slavery all the time. Blair was playing her part perfectly.

"Actually, we are not leaving the galaxy, so it's not really that bad." Peterson wasn't being sarcastic this time, though. He was dead serious. I can't imagine what on earth was wrong with him. We checked our bags and ignored Peterson for the rest of our trip through the airport. As we boarded the plane, I started to realize what I was getting myself into.

"Do you really think this is a good idea?" Blair asked as we took our seats in first class.

"Not at all." I said as I shoved our bags into the overhead compartment.

"Good. I'd be concerned if you did." She chuckled. We sat down in a round booth and Peterson sat in a leather chair across from us.

"I'm assuming that you would like a more detailed explanation for this."

"What an astute observation!" Blair said sarcastically. I could tell Peterson was annoyed with us.

"UIA was originally working with NASA and a few other space stations on interplanetary travel. Three years ago, I was working on lapsing the travel time between Earth and the moon, when I came across a new type of radio frequency that seemed to be the future of immediate travel. When I began testing it using electromagnetic technology, I realized that it didn't have anything to do with time at all. I had actually discovered the technology behind teleportation itself."

"No way!" Blair was astonished. "Are you saying that teleportation has existed for three years, and nobody told us?"

"What kind of an organization are you?" I jumped in. "Aren't you supposed to be helping people?"

"Association, actually." Peterson continued, stirring his tea.

"What?"

"Association. We're not an organization. UIA stands for Universal Intelligence Association.

"Whatever." Blair didn't like smart-mouthed people.

"Anyway, my team and I decided to keep this information from NASA, but it was unfortunately leaked by a friend of mine about six months later." He sounded emotionless as he spoke. "Thankfully, I was able to use the same memory wiping technology on the few who knew about it before it went public."

I can't believe that he was just now explaining all of this. Of course, I didn't believe any of it, but still.

"Why would you want to keep the data from them?" Blair asked.

"The IQ levels that most of the employees at NASA obtained were quite low compared to those on my team. This was concerning because we didn't think that it would be compatible to the more simple-minded. When I hired my team, I had a basic MRI performed on the brain and studied the images carefully."

"I don't think you're allowed to that." I knew that performing those types of procedures was illegal unless you obtained a degree in neurology. I only knew this because Grandpa had told me this when I was younger.

"I studied as a neurologist for several years before obtaining my degree in planetary astronomy." He said flatly. "Will you please save your silly comments for the end?"

"Can you please just relax?" I replied, angry. He rolled his eyes.

"Anyway, as you may know, the average human can only access about ten percent of their brain."

"Everyone knows that." Blair said.

"Well, let's just say that my team wasn't very average. Out of the fifty of us, we each had access to an average of twenty-three percent of our brains."

"That's impossible." Blair and I said in unison. There was no way he was telling the truth.

"Anything is possible." He took a folder from an inner pocket of his sleek, white suit. "Take a look at these." In the folder were MRI images of different angles of the brain. Each one contained the subject's name and basic information such as age, gender, height, weight and a few other things. Each image had one thing in common. The brain was covered in yellow patches.

"What is the yellow for?" Blair asked without looking up.

"It indicates the brain usage levels. If you divide a person's IQ level by ten, the results match the percentage of the brain that has been and is being used."

"How many have been tested?" I asked.

"This discovery was proven, and was released to

NASA and the government only. Since then, everyone in the United States was tested. Seven years ago, all of Earth was tested after world government was notified."

"Even us?"

"Even you."

"How?"

"I don't know if you'll remember this, but at the next doctors visit every individual had since the release, their brains were scanned, and the results were given to UIA."

"Why doesn't the rest of the world know about this?" I asked.

"A meeting was arranged for all world leaders to attend. There, many others and I decided not to notify the less intelligent fraction of the population. Those who did qualify for UIA were to be alerted at eighteen years of age."

"Can we see our results?" Blair asked.

"I thought you would ask that." He pulled out another file. "Here you go."

"Thirty-six percent?" Blair's results were higher than I thought was even possible.

"Miss Davis, do you really think I invited you on this mission because I thought you were strong?" Peterson asked as if she were a little kid.

"Rose, what did you get?" She asked, completely ignoring him. I didn't respond at first. My results couldn't have been accurate. I just stared blankly at my paper. "Rose? What's wrong? What did you get?"

It took me a second to regain my voice. "Forty-three percent."

VIII

"Ladies and gentlemen, this is your pilot speaking. We will now be taking off. Please, buckle your seatbelts and pay attention, as our flight attendants will be giving basic flight emergency information and instructions. Enjoy your flight."

Our flight attendant addressed all of the things we could possibly need to know about our flight.

"Are these your daughters?" she asked Peterson.

"They most certainly are," he lied.

"Well, they are absolutely gorgeous!"

"Thank you," Blair and I said in unison.

"You enjoy your flight, and have fun in Paris!" She walked over to coach.

"Really?" Blair was not happy about this.

"What was I supposed to say? That I just took you from your families and am sending to outer space?"

"That would have been a lot more believable, don't you think?" She snapped.

"Relax. We'll probably never see her again."

"And if you tell that to anyone else, you'll never see the light of day again," she said under her breath.

"So, what do you think of your results?" Peterson asked, trying to change the subject.

"I don't know what to say," I spoke up. "I think this whole thing is crazy." The plane took off.

"Well, there's nothing we can do about it now." Blair said flatly. "What's this 'classified mission' anyway? Does UIA know we're coming?"

"Yes, we've been planning your arrival for

months. We have a vey important job for you."

"How many is 'we'?" I asked.

"UIA? Oh, we've got about thirty thousand by now. If you have an IQ of anything above two-hundred, then you are taken to Europa, like you two."

"How come we weren't brought in at eighteen, like everyone else?" Blair was starting to calm down.

"You two have the highest IQ levels that UIA has ever seen, or even heard of. Blair, with three-hundred and sixty, and Rose, with four-hundred and thirty."

"So?" I knew why this was important, but I asked anyway.

"Take Albert Einstein, or Stephen Hawking for example. Both had an IQ of one hundred and sixty. Famous simply for being pure genius." He was really getting excited. "They changed the world. Now, think of the fact that you are twice as smart as them, with even more advanced technology and teams of people backing you up, helping you change the world!"

Peterson sounded like a good guy with great intentions, but there was still something that I didn't trust about him, Blair saw it too. How on earth could UIA change the world if all they were doing was hiding from it?

"Can I get this lovely family any food or beverages?" The cheerful flight attendant that greeted us a few hours ago walked in holding three menus. "We have some great options on the dinner menu tonight." She passed out the menus and left. "I'll be back in a few!"

"I personally don't fancy airplane food." Peterson said quietly. "However, the French Onion Soup is brilliant."

After about ten minutes, the flight attendant returned.

"Are you ready to order?"

"Yes. Three soups, please." Peterson ordered for us.

"Any special drinks?"

"Girls?" We both shook our heads. "Two waters, and a pot of earl grey. No cream or sugar."

"I'll be right back with that."

Peterson was right. The soup was fantastic. We each devoured our meals and the attendant requested for Blair and me to follow her. She gave us each a pair of silk pajamas and directed us to a small room with two twin beds and a dresser.

"This is fantastic!" Blair said to the attendant.

"There are only four bigger rooms on the plane. This one is a spare, but I thought you could use a little extra comfort. My name is Ella, by the way. You let me know if you need anything at all."

"Thank you." I smiled at her and impulsively gave her a quick hug. "I'm Rose, and this is Blair."

"Absolutely beautiful, you two are. Now, get some rest. Would you like me to wake you up before we land?"

"Yes, please. Will you give us an hour to get ready before landing?" Blair asked politely.

"Of course. See you in the morning." She quietly closed the door and left. We both crawled into bed in our brand new silk pajamas.

"I don't know about you, but I'm keeping these!" Blair smoothed out her periwinkle outfit.

"Great minds think alike." I smiled sadly. I turned off the small lamp that illuminated the cozy room. "Hey," I asked.

"What?'

"Why did you ask Ella to wake us up?"

"So that we would be ready to leave.'

"No! That's not what I meant. We have alarms, you know."

"I know. I just wanted to feel like we had someone else. I feel pretty alone in all of this, even though it's only been a few hours."

"I understand, but maybe she isn't reliable. You heard the police responder on the phone."

"Maybe you're right. But I want all that I can get. Because the truth is I'm scared. I want my years to count,

I want to make something of my life, and I'm afraid that won't happen."

"It will. I promise."

"Goodnight, best friend."

"Goodnight."

IX

I awoke to the sound of knocking on our door.

"Girls. Time to wake up. We land in one hour."

Ella cracked the door open, and I walked over to her.

"How long have we been asleep?"

"Approximately four hours, but little sleep is better than none."

"Agreed." Blair walked over. "Can we please get two cups of coffee?"

"Sure!" She began to write on her notepad. "Would you like cream or sugar with that?"

"Both please. Thank you."

"All right. I'll be back." She closed the door and left.

"Can you believe we're actually in Paris?" I looked out the window at the beautiful city lights below us.

"Pretty crazy." Blair put on a pair of jeans. "What day is it?"

"November twenty seventh."

"You think it will be cold?"

"Yeah, I'd wear a sweater if I were you."

"That's our only option. Our bag is checked, so well have to wear our clothes from yesterday."

"Blair."

"Yeah?"

"I just realized something."

"What?"

"Grandpa died here just a few weeks ago."

"This must be really hard for you, then. I'm so sorry, Rose."

"Yeah. But here's the thing, I don't plan on backing down."

"What do you mean?"

"Being afraid has made me a stronger in a sense. It's always been that way. When my parents died, when I taught myself to drive, when I dropped out of school, when I got a job, always. I refuse to let this be any different."

Silence was the only thing in our cabin for a while. After we did our hair and makeup at the small vanity, Ella walked in with our coffees.

"Sorry it took so long." She carried them on a tray with some sugar, stirring sticks, and cream. "I had a lot of people waiting for breakfast, and then I brewed a fresh pot for you."

"Well, your timing was perfect." Blair said as she took the tray and set it on the desk.

"What's on the breakfast menu?" I asked, sipping my coffee.

"See for yourself." She handed me a small menu. "I recommend the coffee cake muffins, they're amazing."

"The more coffee, the better." Blair pitched in. "We'll have two of those, please."

"Would you like me to bring them to your room or a table?"

"Take them to our dad's table. We'll be there in a moment." Blair was finally playing along. She hated the idea of being Peterson's daughter, but we had no other choice.

"How did you girls sleep?" Peterson was waiting at our booth.

"Fine. You?" I asked as we took our seats.

"Pleasantly. Same dirty clothes, I see." He gestured towards our outfits. He knew we didn't have the option to put on clean clothes, so I don't know what his problem was.

"Same repellant attitude." Blair shot back. I smiled.

"Two coffee cake muffins for two beautiful young ladies." Ella gave us our muffins and refilled our coffee mugs. "You've got about twenty minutes until we land, so I suggest you hurry just a bit."

"Ella, do know what the weather is today?"

"Absolutely. It'll be twenty-three degrees and snowing in Paris today. We will land at approximately two o'clock in the morning New York time, and eight o'clock in the morning Paris time."

"Thanks, Ella." Blair said with a mouth full of food.

"You're most certainly welcome." She skipped away. We finished our breakfast and another attendant picked up our dishes.

"Ladies and gentlemen, this is your pilot speaking." The greeting came over the intercom. "We hope you enjoyed your flight to Paris, France. Today we've got some snowy weather to get you in the holiday mood. You can expect temperatures between twenty and thirty degrees, Fahrenheit, between negative six and one Celsius. We will be landing in five minutes, so please, put away any devices or large items, and tuck any bags beneath your seats. Most importantly, enjoy your destination."

"I thought we were going to Europa. Why Paris?" Blair asked as we began our descent.

"So far, the only teleportation facility on Earth is in Paris. It requires lots of time and money to create such a base. Besides, you can't fly a plane to space in seven hours."

"Obviously, you would need current government permission to build something like that. How could you build it legally without telling them about the whole association?" I asked.

"Every government official on Earth is actually a part of UIA. At the same time the population was tested, all of the current government officials were replaced with those who did qualify for UIA, so that we were able to work on Earth without suspicion."

"But I thought that we voted for our officials," Blair pitched in.

"You do. It's just that there are only qualified candidates that actually run, so you are choosing, but from a specific pool from UIA. We call them the IS, short for Inside Services."

"That makes sense. Will we be working for IS?" I asked.

"Yes, you will." He sounded excited. "You will spend two weeks on Europa, training for your mission. When your time is up, we will send you back to Earth. You will have a deadline to complete your tasks, however I don't think you girls will struggle at all."

"Why, what's the mission?" Blair asked eagerly.

"Let's just say that the Vice President will be receiving a little promotion." I didn't need any extra brainpower to know exactly what was going on.

"You want us to kill the President of the United States?"

X

Before Peterson could respond, it was time to get off the plane. We couldn't talk about it as we walked through the busy airport or in the cab. We were taken to an old museum surrounded by an ugly, dead garden.

"I thought UIA was 'high tech'," Blair said, making little air-quotes with her fingers.

"Yeah." I backed her up. "This place looks like it still uses candles for lighting."

"Wow. You're real talkative, aren't you?" Peterson said under his breath.

"Thanks for noticing!" Blair smiled sarcastically. We walked into the abandoned building. It was falling apart on the inside, nobody was there, and it smelled as if it were full of dead bodies.

"Yeah, so this is probably the nastiest thing I've

ever done," I said as a stepped over a dead rat.

"Patience, girls." Peterson stepped through a pile of broken glass. He led us into a tiny storage closet in the very back of the building.

"I swear, he's trying to kill us." Blair whispered in my ear.

"At least we can't go assassinating people if we're dead." I whispered back.

Peterson turned over what looked like a small titanium cube, and I was surprised to see that it had a built-in screen on the bottom. He placed his finger on the screen and it lit up and scanned his print. He removed his finger, and the screen became a three-dimensional hologram.

"Dang. You weren't lying about the technology, after all." I was completely amazed.

"Nope." He didn't look up from the screen. "These are called NGTs, or Next Generation Technologies. They are very high technology, compact computers designed by our high school students. Most identify you by a fingerprint. You will each be receiving a NGT Watch to use on your mission, and for any other assigned purposes." He finished up with the cube, and the floor opened up, causing Blair and I to scream. We were dropped into a large, white room with illuminated walls. Blair and I stood and brushed ourselves off, but Peterson had no trouble landing on his feet. He led us through an automatic glass door.

"Where are we?" Blair asked, looking around as we walked. We had entered a massive underground facility full of robots, drones, NGTs, and people wearing white suits identical to Peterson's. We walked up to the front desk and a woman wearing the same uniform was typing on her holographic computer screen.

"Allison!" Peterson was happy to see her. "It's been a while!"

"Peterson! Oh my goodness, you brought the girls!" She came out from behind the counter and shook our hands.

"I'm sorry, who are you?" Blair asked.

"Oh, my apologies. My name is Allison Dalton, head of Admission and Recruit Count." She had long, wavy red hair and bright blue eyes. Her body was tall, slender, and covered with freckles. "It's really an honor to meet you!"

"Now, how about we get these girls signed in, Allison?" Peterson tapped on his watch. He didn't wear an NGT watch, which I found quite strange.

"Of course." She walked behind the counter and began typing on her screen again. "Rohana Elizabeth

Walters, will you step up to the camera, please?" She held up a small wireless sphere with a circular lens in the center. I stepped in front of the camera and smiled. She pressed a button on a small square below her computer, and the picture was transferred to the screen.

"What's that for?" Blair asked.

"You'll have a physical and a digital ID here at UIA." Peterson responded. "You'll each be given an ID card that will be able to access anything that is permitted. When new information needs to be added or taken from it, an officer will do so."

"Blair Marie Davis, will you step up to the camera, please?" Blair did so, and we were each handed a card containing our picture, full name, date of birth, weight, and height. It also contained UIA's logo: a series of small hexagons bunched together in a random pattern, which strongly resembled a honeycomb.

"How did you get all of this information?" I asked as I read my card.

"We know everything about everyone." Allison said with a smile. It actually scared me to think that my whole life was being watched. All of my personal data that I myself barely knew was someone's job to keep track of. I could see the worry in Blair's eyes; she was thinking the same thing.

"Let's get to Europa, shall we?" Peterson led us across the lobby into a locked room. He waved his ID card over a sensor by the door. Two men in HAZMAT suits stood behind a row of three large, white pill-shaped tubes. "Well, don't be scared. Just lie down inside a Capsule and relax. You won't feel a thing, I promise." He casually got inside one of the open Capsules and gestured for me to get in one as well.

"Here goes nothing." Blair got in the center

Capsule. I slowly walked over to the tube to the right of hers. I felt beads of sweat running down my back as I lied down. The Capsule was full of little wires, screens and little red and green flashing lights. The two men in the HAZMAT suits walked over and began attaching wires to my hands and forehead. They did the same for Blair and Peterson. I felt like screaming for help as the Capsule door began to close. I've fought claustrophobia since I was little, so this was terrifying for me. For the next ten seconds all I could hear was the sound of my own heartbeat. No lights, no noise, nothing. Then, the Capsule opened. I was in the same white room with the same people.

"Did it work?" Blair asked from beside me.

"Let's find out." I began quickly detaching wires from my body. Blair and Peterson did the same. The men in the HAZMAT suits nodded at Peterson and he unlocked the same vaulted door. It slid open and revealed

a fifty story triangular skyscraper with crystal clear glass

walls. I walked up to the glass and looked out over what

seemed like the entire universe before me. I looked out at

the stars before us. All I could see was endless space.

Peterson spoke from behind me. "Welcome to

Europa."

XI

The station was full of the most insane technology I've ever seen. Robots and drones were buzzing all over the place; there were holograms, computers, and UIA members carrying NGTs as they walked.

"This place is amazing!" Blair exclaimed, focused on the bustle. Everyone wore a tiny pin on his or her black tie. The pin had UIA's logo on it.

"Will we be wearing suits like this?" I asked gesturing towards the members.

"Oh, goodness no!" Peterson laughed. "With the type of work and training you'll have, you'd ruin a suit like that!" he laughed. Blair and I just stared at him blankly. "Oh, you weren't kidding?"

"No, not really." I replied.

"Okay. Uh, how about I show you girls around?" This was getting awkward.

"Sure." Blair said, keen to change the subject.

"For starters, I'd like to let you know that we're not just on some tiny moon." He said as we walked. People left and right were pointing at us and whispering. I wonder why the President was such a threat.

"Europa was actually discovered to have good living conditions. Instead of the harsh climate that you were taught about in school, it actually has the same average humidity and temperature levels as Earth," he continued. Even though there is no alien or plant life because of the lack of oxygen, we decided that this would make a prosperous base."

"Do aliens exist on any planet?" I asked.

"No. Earth is the only planet that supports any

sort of life." Peterson sighed. "The city here is about the size of New York City so far, and we plan on continuing construction in a couple of years."

"Excuse me. City?" Blair looked confused.

"If you weren't so fascinated with the galaxy above us, you would have looked down just a hair." Peterson gestured to the window. We both walked over to the glass. Below us by about ten stories was an amazing city, dozens more skyscrapers, streets, people driving hovering spherical vehicles and motorcycles, and in the midst of it all were Blair and I, the focus of the city around us.

"How is this all possible without any oxygen?" I asked, focused on the people strolling beneath us.

"It's simple, really." Peterson replied. "We've invented a mask that covers the mouth and nose. It is made of only plexiglass, a white foam frame, and a special type of filter. No chords or wires involved. You simply place it on your face and the filter converts anything that is being sucked in into oxygen."

"No way." I didn't believe this; however, I didn't believe in teleportation either, but here we are.

"Now, would you like a complete tour tomorrow, after you are well rested, or would you like to stay late today?"

"What time zone do we follow here?" Blair asked.

"During the teleportation process, your body automatically adapts to the time zone you are teleporting to, so it won't affect your training or other work because your bodies will have good rest even thought you hardly slept." Peterson replied. "If you would really like to know, though, we follow Paris time. That means it is only eleven o'clock in the morning right now. But it really doesn't matter."

"Okay. I think it will be a good idea for Blair and me to go and take in the past events." I said as I placed my hand on her shoulder. "What floor?"

"Floor twenty-nine in building 1543." Peterson said, pulling a slip of paper from his chest pocket. "But I think I'll show you how to use a Cycle, first."

"Cycle?" I asked.

"See those motorcycles down there?" Peterson gestured out the window. "Those are called Cycles. I'll show you how to use one, add the license to your ID, and get you a mask. Once you're all set, you can relax in your apartment, or explore the city."

"Cool! Sounds like a plan to me." Blair walked

towards an elevator and Peterson and I followed. We made our way to the basement level that looked like a baggage claim area at an airport. There were two sleek, black a Cycles with neon blue accents by a set of two vaulted glass doors. They had no tires, just a hollow base with a neon blue stripe lining the inside of the circle. The black paint had a matte finish, and above the blue handlebars was an NGT screen and a glass windshield.

"You can give it a test run down here. Have you ever ridden a motorcycle?" Peterson asked.

"Nope." I began to mount the Cycle when Peterson picked me up from behind and set me down on the concrete floor.

"Hold your horses!" He said with a chuckle. "It'll take some basic knowledge to use these."

"I think we already have enough of that." Blair

said as she and I began to get on the vehicles once again. I scanned my card on the NGT screen and it added the license number below my name. The screen popped up into a hologram and stated a few main ideas of the Cycle. I read through them quickly. It was mostly just basic stuff like my ID is the only one that can activate my Cycle, and work the built-in NGT. I looked over how to use the buttons and codes and I understood immediately. Blair took off next to me. I pressed the hologram and the Cycle turned on, the engine was silent, but I could still tell because the Cycle had begun to hover about a five inches above the ground.

"I would ask how this is possible, but I think I'll just go." I waved to Peterson and followed Blair. By the time we were completely familiar with driving our new vehicles around the room, Peterson gave us two masks.

"These are what keep you alive outside." He

spoke in a serious tone. "You won't be receiving any replacements or repairs, so I suggest you keep them in good condition." The masks looked like clear ski goggles that cover a person's mouth and nose instead of eyes. They had a white plexigalss frame lined with foam.

"How do they stay on?" I asked. The mask didn't have a strap to wrap around my head.

"Like this." Peterson took the mask from my hands and placed it over my mouth and nose. "This button here turns it on." He pressed a small button on the outer frame. The mask suctioned to my face and cut of my air supply completely. I started to panic and tried to remove the mask, but it wouldn't budge. Peterson grabbed my shoulders and pressed another button. "And this one gives you air." He rolled hid eyes. I was able to breathe again and calmed myself down. Somehow, I could easily speak with the mask on.

"You could have killed me!" I was still pretty panicked over the whole situation.

"Oh, relax. You're fine." Peterson said as he adjusted Blair's mask. I don't think that he understands that we're technically still kids. We've been sent to Paris with a stranger who erased six hours worth of crucial memories from our families, told that we are geniuses assigned to kill the President, and then teleported to Europa. This was not a joke to Blair and me. Peterson, on the other hand, didn't seem to mind much. "You're free to go." He said. "Walk through the first set of doors and scan your ID on the NGT screen to your right. The doors behind you will seal off and after about five seconds, the second set will open. Once they do, you can hop on your Cycles and head to your apartment buildings. Sign in at the lobby and your apartment key and address will be added to your ID. Call me if you need anything," he said blankly as he handed me a slip of paper with an NGT contact number on it.

"When will we get our NGTs?" Blair asked.

"Oh! Thank you for reminding me." Peterson took two sleek white watches from his front pocket. "Here you go. You can activate them when you get home."

"Thanks." I took one of the watches.

"Let's head out." Blair said and she put on her watch and got on her Cycle. We slowly rode into the first set of doors and they sealed behind us, sucking all the air out. The second set of doors opened and we rode out to the busy streets.

"This is amazing!" I exclaimed.

"No kidding! And so beautiful, too!" Blair shouted back.

"Lets ride around for a bit before we get to the apartment." We checked out the beautiful sculptures and buildings, all unique. We rode to building 1543 and checked in at the front desk. We rode up a glass elevator to floor twenty-nine. I thought about what I was really here for. Was it worth it? It was dangerous and filled me with dread.

We entered the two-story modern penthouse filled with furs and works of modern art. There were three bedroom, four bathrooms, and a closed balcony that overlooked the city. Blair and I unpacked and sat down on a large white sofa. When I sat down, the cushion below me made a crinkling noise.

"What's that?" Blair asked as I pulled out an envelope from underneath my seat.

"Let's find out." I opened up the envelope and pulled out a tiny slip of paper.

"What's it say?"

"It's all a lie." I read the typed lettering. "Run."

XII

I woke up the next morning and grabbed my watch. It was full of messages from unknown numbers simply telling me to run. I ignored them and got ready for the day. I put on a long blue gown that I don't remember packing. I don't know why I decided to wear something so elaborate, before I left my room I looked out my window. The streets were completely empty. No light was visible, I could hardly see around me. It wasn't what I was expecting from a big city at all. I walked downstairs and made myself some breakfast. Blair was nowhere to be found.

"Blair!" I yelled. "Where are you? It's time to leave!" I searched the penthouse but there was no trace of her anywhere.

"Right here!" She yelled. I couldn't tell what direction her muffled voice was coming from. "Just a minute!"

I sat down, still unsure of where exactly everyone was.

"Okay, just hurry!" I finished began my breakfast in the empty room. I heard nothing but my own heartbeat. I was about to stand when all of the sudden a cold pair of hands secured my wrists behind my back. I turned around to see Blair. I sighed in relief.

"Run." She sat down next to me.

"What?"

"It's all a lie. Run." She casually cut up a peach and started eating. "Run."

"Blair, what's going on with you?" I backed away from her.

"I said run! Okay? Go, get out of here!" Her eyes

were bloodshot and she began to laugh hysterically. "It's a lie! It's all one big lie! Run!" She stepped on the skirt of my blue gown and ripped it down the center. She didn't look like she was going crazy, she was scared. She wanted to protect me, but it was horrible. I began to scream as she shook my shoulders. "Run! Please! Rose, Rose! Rose, wake up! Rose, wake run! Wake up!" She was telling me to wake up, so I did. It was all a dream.

"What happened?" She was standing over me, grabbing my shoulders. "You were screaming your lungs out!" She helped me sit up.

"I had a horrible dream about the note... and you attacked me." I was covered in sweat and tears, shaking all over. "You kept telling me to run."

"Hey, it's okay. Everything is going to be fine. That will never happen, I promise." Blair led me downstairs to the couch and gave me a blanket and some fresh hot coffee. She sat down next to me and gave me a hug. "Now, I want you to tell me what happened, but just relax."

"Okay." My breathing slowed down and I told Blair everything that happened. When we were younger, just after my parents died, I had horrible nightmares every night. For about eight months straight, Blair would call me every morning and tell me everything was going to be okay. Even on days she was busy, or if she were going to see me that day anyway, she would call me.

"Listen, I got your back." She hugged me again. "No matter what happens, I'm always here for you. You can count on me."

"Thank you." I hugged her back. We finished our breakfast and got dressed. I put on a pair of black jeans and a white cropped hoodie. Blair wore a black sleeveless blouse and some white jeans. We did our hair and makeup, and I put on the pearl necklace that I wore to Grandpa's funeral.

"Hey, great minds think alike!" Blair chuckled when she saw my black and white outfit.

"I know, right?" I started to walk over to my watch, which had been buzzing. I opened my messages, and thankfully, nobody was telling me to run.

"What's up?" Blair asked, hopping off of the sofa.

"It's Peterson."

"Oh, no! We were supposed to be at Headquarters, weren't we?"

"Yeah, but thankfully, he said he'll meet us here in about fifteen minutes with our gear. Apparently he had something come up, so we have the day off."

"Oh, cool. I almost went into cardiac arrest there." Blair jokingly wiped her forehead. We just blankly stared at each other for a few seconds and then started laughing.

"Okay, okay." I said in between breaths. "We should probably clean up now."

"Yeah, Peterson will be here any minute." We fixed all of the pillows and put away the dirty dishes. Just when we had finished, there was a knock on the door.

"Come in!" I shouted as I straightened my shirt. Peterson walked in the door carrying two grey duffel bags and handed one to each of us.

"Good morning!" He sounded nervous. "Say, you didn't see anything strange last night, did you?" He faked a smile and rubbed his hands together. I looked back at Blair, who was now in the kitchen. She had a look of suspicion on her face and quickly shook her head.

"No, why?" I tried my hardest to sound innocent.

"Oh, no reason." He changed the subject. "So, how was your first night?"

"Great!" Blair walked back over to us, holding her duffel. "What's in here?"

"That bag contains all of your training supplies." He replied.

"Like what?" I asked.

"For starters, your uniform. I'll explain it to you in a minute." He made his way to the sofa, and to my surprise, looked under the cushions. Blair and I put the envelope the exact same spot we found it last night, to avoid suspicion. When he came across it, he was quick to stuff it into his pocket.

"What was that?" Blair asked. She and I had the same idea.

"Oh, sometimes people leave trash that isn't found by our janitors." His tone reminded me of Alex at the café. He didn't sound like he was even trying to be convincing.

"Uh huh." Blair opened her duffel and began to browse through her items. She pulled out a black, skintight bodysuit made from an extremely flexible fabric. "Sweet! Rose, get yours out." I pulled the suit from my bag and held it up over my body.

"Go on then, try them on." Peterson smiled. Blair and I went upstairs and changed into the suits. We walked back down the spiral staircase.

"How do they fit so perfectly?" I asked.

"The mixture of materials used in the suit make it

flexible, weightless, and best of all, bulletproof. It is designed to automatically conform to whoever is wearing it."

"Bulletproof?" Blair and I asked in unison.

"You'll still receive damage from any shots, however no permanent or deadly injury will be inflicted."

"That's amazing." Blair ran her fingers up and down her thin sleeve.

"It most certainly is amazing," he replied. "By the way, the rest of your supplies must be brought to training, and you are required to be wearing your suits."

"Every day?" Blair looked up. "Don't we have to wash them or something?"

"Of course." He chuckled. "You have two suits each. Your next one will be delivered tomorrow."

"Oh, cool. So, what else is in here?" I asked as I rummaged through the contents.

"Pistols, practice ammunition, gym shoes, strychnine powder, and a couple other things. You need to be equipped with these items every day."

"Strychnine?" Blair continued to look through her bag. I froze. Strychnine. Only a fraction of a gram ingested will immediately cut off and confuse nerves and muscles. My chemistry teacher showed us the reaction of the deadly powder by injecting a toad with it. The whole nervous system goes down, resulting in spasms and cramps. Eventually the lungs shut down and that's it. I looked up at Peterson.

"Listen, I need to go," he looked at his watch. "I'll have your Training Manager explain everything, okay?"

"Who's she? The Training Manager, I mean."

"He, actually. His name is Alexander Price." He walked out the door. "Goodbye!"

XIII

I could tell Blair wasn't happy. Alex could've literally stopped all of this. If he would have just told me about the upcoming bombs, instead of acting like he was too good to give me an explanation, I would have left and none of this would have happened. I could never forgive him after I saw poor little Mia covered in ash and Grandma's broken ankle. Now, I'm technically under his command.

"You know what?" Blair took a deep breath and her expression cooled down. "I almost forgot that today is National Best Friend Day."

"No it's not." I said.

"It is now, and we are going out to dinner."

"Dinner? It's not even noon."

"Then we'll go to lunch, and have brownies for

dinner."

"Because that's so healthy," I laughed. We changed back into our original outfits and grabbed our purses. I was glad that Blair didn't go on a rant about this. We both needed a break, anyway. "How do we find a restaurant?" I asked. "Everything looks so different here."

"I'll look on my watch." Blair began typing. We played around with our watches last night. I also practiced using my oxygen mask. Now we're pretty familiar with the way they work. "Got it," She showed my the hologram. "Do burgers sound good?"

"Yes! Send the directions to your Cycle."

"Already ahead of you."

"I'm honestly surprised that people here eat the same food as we do on Earth. Is that weird?" We walked into the cold parking garage.

"Nope, I am too."

"I was expecting some crazy organic zero-gravity vegetable juice," I put on my mask and thankfully did not suffocate myself this time. We got on our Cycles and rode out of the airtight passage and to the restaurant. Every building here on Europa has a small parking garage underneath it, which makes navigation a little confusing. When we walked through the doors to the restaurant, I was not at all surprised to see that everything had the same modern theme.

"This is neat." Blair said.

"Yeah, it's nice."

"Hey, you're the new heroes, aren't you?" A dark skinned boy, about our age walked up to us carrying some menus and a tray of empty cups.

"Well, I wouldn't say heroes," Blair twiddled her

thumbs behind her back. I could tell right away that she liked him, but I didn't say anything.

"Really? Cause I'm pretty sure I've heard every rumor around about two lovely young recruits coming to save all of us."

"You know what? You're right, that is us." I jumped in. "You must be a genius. Can we get a booth by a window, please?"

"Sure." He smiled shyly at Blair. "Just follow me." He led us to a booth right on a glass wall, and gave us two menus.

"Something doesn't feel right." I put my menu down after about five minutes of staring at it, completely zoned out.

"Well, we've been shipped to another planet, told we are complete geniuses, and assigned to kill the

President of the United States for classified reasons."
Blair said blankly. "What could possibly be wrong?"

"No, really. Do you remember how Peterson told
us that every government official on Earth is a part of
UIA?"

"So?"

"We've been given a mission to kill the
President, who must be a very highly ranked member of
UIA, who must have also been cut off. Otherwise he
would know about the mission. I mean, our waiter
instantly recognized us, so this is obviously very public."

"I never thought of it that way." Blair stopped
reading the menu.

"And the note telling us to run, who could have
sent that?"

"Wait. Why wouldn't UIA, with all of their

technology and thousands of members, just kill the president themselves? Why train two teenagers for two whole weeks to do it for them?"

"Good point. There's definitely more to this than we're being told."

"I have an idea." She picked up her menu and began going on and on about one of the burgers.

"What are you doing?" I was totally confused.

"Just play it cool." She whispered. The same guy that greeted us walked over to our table carrying a notepad and pen.

"You ladies ready to order?"

"Yes, I'll have the Classic, please," she smiled.

"Me, too." I obviously sounded confused, judging by the look she shot me.

"All right, two Classics coming right up." He began to walk away, but Blair interrupted.

"Excuse me, sir."

"Yeah? My name is Oliver, by the way."

"Oh, sorry. Oliver, what do you think of our mission? I mean, do you think the IS supports the whole thing? The president, especially." Blair was always one to be sneaky, but this was downright genius.

"IS?" he raised an eyebrow.

"Inside Services," I specified.

"Oh, yeah. To be honest, I don't really know much about the President's personal thoughts, but I know that he, and the entire IS, are really proud of you girls."

"And what do you know if the mission? We didn't know that it would be this public, that's for sure."

"The most that we ordinary citizens know is that you'll be helping test the next generation for IQ. Other than that, no other info was released to the public," he smiled.

I couldn't believe what I had just heard. This was exactly the opposite of what we were told. In fact, if any information was actually released to the public, it was a lie if I didn't know any better.

"That's right, were helping UIA's population grow!" I smiled the most innocently I possibly could. "We are so honored to find the next generation of geniuses to change the world."

"Great! Can't wait to see what you've got coming." Oliver walked off to another table across the room.

"That's it. I'm calling Peterson." I pulled out my

NGT.

"Wait. Not here. Let's wait until we get home, then we can have him over for dinner. We can have a real conversation then." Blair was just as upset as I was.

"I thought we were having brownies for dinner."

"Oh, yeah. Well we just won't share, then."

"Okay." I messaged Peterson inviting him to a meeting.

"Here you go." Oliver walked over carrying two full plates of food.

"This looks amazing!" Blair's face lit up.

"Thanks. I'll be sure to tell the chef. Do you need anything else?"

"No, I think we're okay." I nodded.

"Enjoy." We finished eating and paid for our meal. Blair paid with her NGT. We hurried out and got home as soon as we could.

"What now?" I asked. "Peterson isn't supposed to be here for another five hours."

"We can figure something out."

"Hey, you never did answer my question about the note. What do you think it means?"

"I think we've figured out the lie by now. The only problem is that we can't run from any of it."

XIV

Blair and I talked about the day's events for a couple of hours and then we both fell asleep. I woke up about half an hour before Peterson said he would be here and woke Blair up, too. When he knocked on the door I was ready to answer.

"Hello, ladies. It was very kind of you to invite me over like this." He walked in the door right past Blair and me. "Especially on your first full day here."

"We need to talk," Blair pulled out a chair at the table, gesturing for him to sit. He did and Blair and I sat across from him.

"Let's get one thing straight," I looked him dead in the eye. "We're not playing your games. You're going to answer our questions and stay on subject or we're not completing this mission. Understand?"

"I was expecting this," he sighed.

"What?"

"You two aren't the type to host a friendly gathering, are you?"

"This gathering would be friendly if you weren't lying to us and keeping secrets," Blair said.

"Excuse me? What secrets, and what lies?"

"Oh, just the usual," I said sarcastically. "Lying to the public about the mission, or maybe even lying to us. At this point there are so many lies that I can't figure out what the real lie really is!"

"Okay, so maybe I didn't tell the public about the real mission. I promise you, it was for your own safety, though."

"This entire thing is the exact opposite of safe,"

Blair commented.

"Were not doing anything you say until we can get a good explanation," I said.

"Okay, what do you need to know?"

"Just give us a layout of the whole mission, and good reasons," Blair said. "Stay on subject!"

"Fine," he shrugged, "a lot of the mission is classified to you, though, and so I can only give certain information."

"You're your own boss," I interrupted, "whatever is classified was classified by you. I'm pretty sure you can tell us."

"I'll tell you what I'm willing to tell you, nothing more."

"Just hurry up, will you?" Blair rolled her eyes.

"Fine, fine. Your deadline to complete the mission is December thirteenth, no later. You'll spend two weeks here training in three different main divisions; stealth, agility, and advanced combat."

"Advanced combat?" I asked, "How hard can this mission possibly be?"

"Oh, really it's not that big of a deal," he said sarcastically. "You've just got to strut on past the Secret Service guards, disable all of the high tech security cameras, and get past the laser technology borders sown through practically every hallway in the White House. Easy." He smiled.

"Can't you just shut all of that down and tell the guards to let us in?" I had finally found a loophole.

"I could, but I won't."

"Why?"

"I can't tell anyone that we're doing this, only the three of us know. It had better stay that way, too."

"And why couldn't you just kill the president yourself instead of hauling us here? Couldn't you ask members of UIA?" Blair asked.

"Classified," He looked down at his watch and simply left the penthouse without another word.

"Classified," Blair mocked him.

"This is absolutely ridiculous!" I yelled.

"I agree," Blair said. "We can't just sit around and follow orders like puppets."

"I don't plan on it," I said.

"Hey, maybe we can ask Alex tomorrow. I'm sure he'll tell us what's up."

"Alex is the last person I want to see right now."

"Well, he also seems to be the last person that knows enough to give us the information we need."

"Good point."

"I'm always right," She started typing on her NGT watch. "Here, I found his ID," she pulled up the holographic screen. "Alexander Price, no middle name, I guess. His contact number is 3673."

"I'll add him to my messages. Meanwhile, we have brownies to make."

XV

Blair is the most amazing person I've ever met. Even with all that's happened over the past two weeks, Grandpa's death, the bombing, Alex, Peterson, and the mission, I feel safe. I may be on a far away moon in a secret base, but I still feel at home with her. And even though it's been a stressful day, here we are, making brownies for dinner. Why? Because that's what best friends are for. I don't know what I would do if I lost Blair. That's why my main priority in the middle of this mess is to make sure we get home safely. Especially her.

"Should we really be doing this?" She asked as she wiped the counter top.

"Doing what?" I chuckled. I put the pan of batter into the oven and set the timer.

"Eating brownies for dinner right before we train to be undercover assassins."

"Oh, that? Yeah, probably not."

"No, really. I'm worried about this, Rose. I mean, we're only seventeen. How could someone possibly expect us to do this?"

"I don't know," the doorbell ringing cut me off. I walked over to the door yelling, "I'm coming. I'm coming!" I opened the door, and was surprised to see that nobody was there.

"That's weird," Blair walked over to me and looked around the hallway. "Nothing's here."

"Wait," I bent down and picked up a small sheet of paper that was stuffed under the hinge of the door. It was another note telling us that it is all a lie and that we should run.

"What's it say this time?"

"Same thing as last time. Nothing has changed.

Same size, same typewriter font, same message, everything is an exact replica. I wonder if anyone else is getting these."

"Well, if someone wants us to get out of here, Peterson must know about it, judging by his reaction last time."

"You're right. But who, and why?"

"Remember it said that 'It's all a lie'. The real question is what is 'it'?"

"I'm guessing all of this stuff with UIA."

"I don't know, Peterson sounded pretty serious. He even showed us real diagrams. Plus, why would he make us do this as a joke?"

"Let's write back," I shrugged.

"Excuse me?"

"Let's write back. I mean, why not?"

"If Peterson knew about the last note, he'll know about this one, too. In fact, I'll bet the reason he left out of the blue was because he knew someone was going to, or already did, drop it off."

"I see your point," There was a long pause. "How else will we find out about this, though?"

"I don't know," I could see hopelessness building up in her face. "I just want to go home."

"Me too; but we can't. There's nothing we can do."

"Why not? Why not just tell Peterson we're not going through with this?"

"He won't let us leave, I guarantee; but hey, let's look on the bright side. It'll be a lot more fun punching Peterson after his own recruitment staff shows you how." She looked at me as if I were entirely insane for a second, and I completely regretted what I had just said. "Oh, I didn't mean it like that." Just when I thought I couldn't make things any worse, she started cracking up.

"You're totally right!" She said while laughing. I was so relieved at her reaction, that I started laughing, too. There's another thing I love about Blair, her optimism. We finally stopped laughing when the oven went off. Our brownies were done.

"Hey," Blair said as she took a sip of milk, "I'm sorry." I didn't know exactly what she was sorry for, but I didn't ask.

"Me too," I said. We sat in silence for a while, admiring the city below us. Just as I was about to get another brownie, my watch went off.

"Who is it?" Blair asked.

"Alex," I rolled my eyes, "he wants to let us know that

we need to show up fifteen minutes early."

"I'll set my alarm for five in the morning."

"Sounds good, I'll do the same."

"Whoa! It's already ten o'clock! We should get to bed."

"For sure!" We both got ready for bed and organized our things for training the next day. I should have gotten plenty of sleep, but I only got a couple of hours. I was too busy thinking about the note. Peterson knows about them, for sure. He's keeping secrets; and if he's not willing to tell us anything, I will do whatever I can to find out myself.

XVI

I was disappointed when my alarm went off. I barely slept at all. I was up almost all night thinking, and I really wish I had let myself sleep. I heard Blair's alarm going off across the hall and crawled out of bed. As I double-checked the contents of my bag, I opened up my blinds and looked at the magnificent city below. I can't say that it was still dark outside, because the sky is always dark here, but the city lights always give off such a glow that it looks like day from the streets. I was happy to see that there were already hovering vehicles, pedestrians, open shops, and full restaurants. The city never sleeps here, but I am used to it because New York City is no different. I heard knocking on my door.

"I'll start on breakfast!" Blair called from the hall.

"Thanks," I replied, "I'll be down in a minute!" I

put on my new suit and shoes, tied my hair up, and walked downstairs.

"Here you go," Blair handed me a sliced peach from the almost empty fruit basket. The only food that came with the penthouse was the peaches, probably just for decoration. We had to order the ingredients to make brownies yesterday, and we probably should have also considered some real food while we were at it. I didn't feel like going shopping last night, and I still don't, but it has to be done.

"Let's go back to that burger place for lunch today," I said.

"Good idea. I liked it there."

"We should also find some time after training to go to the grocery store," I added. "We need some real food here."

"For sure," she nodded. We both finished eating and Blair looked at her watch. "Hey, it's five-thirty, we should probably head out now."

"You're right. Do you have your bag?" She was dressed the same as I was, so I didn't doubt that she would: however, the last thing we needed today was to be unprepared.

"Yeah, I've got everything."

"Good. Let's get out of here." We got on our Cycles and drove to the Training Center, right next to Headquarters. The building was an opaque black skyscraper. It was round and covered in reflective material. The building was really quite beautiful. We rode up the elevator from the garage and into the lobby. I walked to the front desk, hiding my face. Many people knew our faces very well here. Most would point us out and whisper to each other, while glancing constantly.

Some people would love this kind of attention, but I didn't. Neither did Blair. I rushed up to the front desk while trying to avoid eye contact with any of the others in the lobby. I was surprised to see Allison, the woman from Paris, at the desk waiting eagerly for us.

"Allison?" Blair looked up, "What are you doing here? I thought you worked in Paris."

"I do, actually." She briefly hugged us. "Peterson thought it would be best for me to take you to your station on your first day. To avoid all of the commotion, you know." She spoke just as an ordinary adult would talk to their friends or family. I liked that about Allison. She didn't treat us like babies. That's all I want now; I just want to feel normal again. "Let's get upstairs, then. Shall we?" We followed her into an elevator and almost instantly made our way to the twenty-seventh floor. We were lead into a massive, several-story room full of unique weapons, platforms, outfits, and shelves full of high tech pieces that were too elaborate to describe. The one thing that made the room stand out from the rest of UIA's buildings was that there wasn't a person in sight. There wasn't even the faintest sound anywhere. This whole thing was meant for me and Blair alone. The idea scared and excited me all at the same time.

The three-story station was tall and circular. The first and second floors only came out about ten feet from the round walls, creating an empty space in the center, which reached from the floor to the ceiling. Each floor was about fifteen feet high, except for the third, which was at least twenty feet. There was a huge skylight in the ceiling, with an elaborate hanging light fixture in the center; it was a series of three-dimensional hexagons hanging in the same pattern as UIA's logo. The second floor, which we entered on, was full of displays containing weapons and gadgets. The first floor was not a loft. It had two round elevated platforms in the center. The walls were lined with several rows of suits and high tech accessories. There was another round platform in the center of the room, level with the third floor. It was connected to the floor of the highest loft by four walkways, one on each quadrant. Because of the extra platform, it was hard to see what was up there. Two elevators on either side of the room were the only access from floor to floor. Everything was perfectly tied together.

"You girls can look around for a little bit." Alex walked in behind us. He was wearing the same suit as Blair and I were.

"Okay, we will. Thanks," Blair said.

Alex walked out of the room, and the sliding doors shut behind him. He was having some sort of conversation with Allison. Blair and I waited about five minutes without talking or moving around at all. I didn't think he'd take this long.

"Hey," I finally spoke up. "Alex said we could look around. Let's take advantage of that while we can."

"Sure," she opened up her bag.

"That's not what I meant," I chuckled.

"I know. But I wanted to show you this first," she took a small pouch from the bottom of the duffel. It was full of small vials containing a fine white powder. "What's it for?"

Then it hit me; Blair had no idea what Strychnine was. "No idea," I lied. I opened up my bag to find the same pouch, containing the same powders. "I'm sure Alex will explain them." I was afraid to tell her myself, so I acted confused, too.

"Yeah," Blair put the vials away. "Let's look

around now." Just as we moved over to the wall of shelves, Alex walked in.

"Welcome to Europa," he put his hand out to shake mine.

"Thank you, Mr. Price," I smiled and shook his hand.

"Oh please, Miss Walters," he pulled his hand away, "call me Alex."

"It's Rose, actually."

"And I'm assuming you'd prefer to be called Blair," he turned to shake Blair's hand, but she refused the offer.

"How about we just start." She said.

"Okay, would you like a tour?"

"No."

"All right, let's head to base three," he led us into one of the elevators and we shot to the top. "Before I get you into handling any weapons I'd like to do a skills test."

The doors opened to reveal a completely empty loft and center platform. We crossed the walkway to the platform. None of the lofts had any sort of rails, so it would be easy to fall off if you weren't paying attention.

"Basically, just try and pin me down for more than three seconds. You can do anything you deem necessary to keep me down, and I can retaliate."

"That's too easy," I spoke up, "there's got to be some sort of catch."

"Sure there is. I thought it would be more obvious to such a smart girl like you," he raised an eyebrow, then gave a mischievous look. "You see, I'm an agent trained specifically in the field of combat. And, well, you're just a little girl." This comment made me angrier than I could even describe. He was right though, I don't know a thing about combat, but I'm no little girl.

"Oh yeah?" I stepped into the center of the platform. "Try me."

XVII

It didn't take me long to realize I'd made a mistake. Sure I've dodged bombs before, but this actually seemed more dangerous. Of course Alex wouldn't be allowed to hurt me though. Would he? I mean, I am very valuable to the association. Peterson would have Alex fired at the very least if I was unable to complete the mission, especially if it was because of him.

"You know, Rose," Alex slowly approached the platform, "I've noticed something about you that really stands out to me."

"Oh really?" I stayed alert. "And what's that?"

"You are a very driven person."

"I prefer the term passionate."

"And what would you say your passion is for?"

"A lot of things, but today I'm most interested in

revenge," I stepped in front of him, grabbed his wrists, and knocked his legs out from underneath his body. He hit the ground hard, landing on his back. "That's for almost killing my family!"

"Dang," Blair spoke from the loft. "Definitely didn't see that one coming."

"Yeah," Alex winced as he stood up. "Me neither. It wasn't my idea, though. The bombs. So technically you cant blame me."

"Who's idea was it, then?" I asked fiercely.

"I don't know, I got an anonymous message," he was lying. I decided not to question him any further since I knew it was probably Peterson, anyway. But why?

"Fine, did I at least pass the test?"

"This isn't necessarily a 'passing' type of test, its more of a way to see where you sit on the scale as far as combat skills," he brushed himself off. "I will be sure to put you in a more advanced starting level."

"Okay," I looked over my shoulder, "and what about Blair?"

"I'll put her with you."

"Don't you want to test me, too?" Blair spoke up and walked over.

"Technically, yes. But-" he was cut off by another blow from Blair. She kicked his legs out too, causing him to fall again.

"Done," she helped him up this time. "Let's continue."

"I really wasn't expecting this," he led us to the bottom floor, slightly limping.

"Expecting what?" I asked.

"I don't know, I just thought you'd be really nervous or something." His limp was gone by now. I didn't feel bad.

"Yeah right," I laughed. "The girl who has been living independently, has a full time job, a little sister to feed and educate, and her own apartment is going to be scared of taking on a little boy," I smirked. "Not to mention the fact that I am quite successful in life and will soon be receiving a nice promotion. Oh yeah, and I ran through a field of active bombs to save my family. I'm definitely terrified."

"She has a point," Blair nudged Alex as he typed a code into his NGT. "Rose doesn't mess around."

"Okay, and what about you?" he asked Blair.

"My dad passed away when I was fifteen. I take care of my mom, pay the bills, go to night school five days a week, and work a day job from Monday to Thursday. On Fridays, I babysit Mia. I may not have it too bad, but I don't live a luxurious life."

"Who's Mia?"

"My little sister," I said. "Don't you remember her from the café?"

"Oh yeah," he typed in one last code and the platforms in the center of the room lit up. "Step right up."

"What's this for?" Blair asked as Alex handed her a small gun.

"You're on a mission to kill," he handed me the same gun. "How else are you supposed to get the job done?"

"Haven't you thought this through?" Blair laughed.

"Yes?"

"If someone hears a gun go off in the middle of the night, in the President's room, in the White House, don't you think we'll blow our cover just a little bit?"

"No."

"Have you ever heard a gun fire?"

"Yes. Have you ever heard *this* gun fire?"

"No."

"Exactly! And you never will. Because they're silent."

"That's impossible," I spoke up.

"Yeah," he chuckled, "So is teleportation."

After I saw the strychnine, I assumed Peterson expected us to poison the President. Why were we doing this?

"Fine," Blair aimed, pulled the trigger, the gun fired, perfect shot, no sound.

"Rose?" He gestured for me to shoot.

"No."

"Excuse me?"

"I said no. I'm not shooting anyone. Especially not my President."

"The guns will only be used for self defense."

"Okay, then," I shot the gun. Perfect accuracy. There wasn't even backfire. My dad taught me to shoot when I was younger in case of an emergency. I guess I never forgot how.

"How are we going to kill President Voltaire, then?" Blair asked, putting the gun away. "You implied that this was our only option."

"Poison."

"The white powders?"

"Yes, just slip one vial into his bedside drink."

"That's it?"

"That's it, just a painless process. Then you can go back home and forget all of this," Alex looked up at me. He knew he lied, and he knew that I understood that it would be anything but painless. He knew that this wasn't fair. He knew that it was illogical and unreasonable to do this to innocent people. Did he? Maybe Peterson lied to him, too. Even if he did though, I'm sure Alex would've been smart enough to see the truth.

"So, what's our agenda for today?" I asked.

"Just an introduction. Skills tests for physical combat skills, weaponry skills, and technology skills."

"Technology?" Blair asked. "How do we test for that?"

"It's pretty easy," he explained," I'll just show you how to use a few basic gadgets you'll have on the mission. If by the end of the next two weeks, you know how to use all of your gadgets, you pass."

There were a few gadgets we'd be using. Most of them were just basic technology such as communication microphones and earpieces that connected to our NGTs through Bluetooth. The earpiece allowed Blair and me to hear each other, and they also enhanced other sounds. A laser was built into the piece; if you pointed it at someone, it would somehow amplify any of the noise it made. Basically, we now had the ability to eavesdrop on anyone's conversations. I figured this was pretty cool, but it also put me even more on edge. What if the same technology was being used on me? The microphone was easy to understand. We could whisper into it and anyone on the other end would get the message. The reason they connected to the NGTs Bluetooth was to allow our conversations to be monitored. If we were in trouble, Alex would know. They could be used without the Bluetooth, but it was required. We worked on a few other things and the time flew by.

"It's lunch time," Alex checked his watch.

"See you in an hour!" Blair and I were already halfway out the door, starving. We got in our Cycles and rode to the restaurant that we went to a few days before. The name was '8645129'. None of the businesses other than Headquarters and the Training Center had names. Instead, they had identification numbers. We decided to call the restaurant 'Eighty-Six'.

"Welcome back," Oliver, the boy from our first visit was surprised to see us. Blair greeted him kindly, but

I didn't pay attention. I was too focused on Peterson. He was sitting at a table on the glass wall, talking to Allison, who probably should've been back in Paris. Peterson didn't seem like his usual self, though. He was furious. Contained, but furious. I had to know what was going on.

"Excuse me," I finally spoke. "Can we get a table behind the man in the white suit? I do enjoy the view from there."

XVIII

Apparently the only table next to Peterson was reserved, so we sat at the bar.

"Here you go," Oliver handed me a menu. "I'll be back in a minute." He walked away and I turned to Blair.

"Hey," I whispered, "try and listen to Peterson. He seems really angry with Allison."

"What are you talking about?" "I don't see either of them."

"They're behind us at the window, where we sat yesterday." Blair turned her head. "No," I stopped her, "we don't want to look suspicious. Try to make sure he doesn't see you."

"Okay, I guess. Hey! Use your earpiece, but turn the Bluetooth off."

I remembered when Alex made it very clear that

we weren't allowed to take the Bluetooth off, but I didn't care. He didn't give any reason, and its not like he would find out anyway.

"Good idea, I pulled out the earpiece and focused it between the two. It worked. I heard just mumbling at first, then it cleared up.

"I can't do that, sir," Allison said. She sounded irritated.

"You can and you *will*," Peterson retorted.

"With all due respect, what you're asking me to do is illogical. You haven't even given me a good reason."

"Yes, I did, Allison. The nitrogen levels are unhealthy and children younger than seventeen should not be here. They must be sent to Earth by tomorrow."

"You don't have proof."

"You don't need proof! Last I checked I'm your boss. You do what I tell you to do! You will have the children out of here by tomorrow night or, I'll have to replace you! Understood?"

"Yes, sir," Allison walked out. Peterson paid the bill and left as well. Thankfully, neither of them saw us.

"So?" Blair asked.

"Peterson wants all children sixteen and under sent to Earth by tomorrow because the air conditions are unhealthy. Allison said he has no proof and told him she wouldn't do it. Peterson almost lost it and said he'll fire her if she doesn't finish the job by tomorrow night. She agreed."

"I bet he doesn't have proof."

"Me too," I said. It was all so strange.

"It wouldn't make any sense for Peterson to do

this, though. The children have done nothing to him, and they couldn't possibly have gotten in the way of our mission."

"That's what I was thinking," I was about to call Alex when Oliver came to the table.

"Hello, are you ready to order?"

"Yes, we are," Blair handed him her menu. "I'll have the Classic again, with sweet potato fries, please."

"And I'll have the Original with grilled vegetables. Thank you," I handed him my menu and he walked away.

"So what do you think about training so far?" Blair asked.

"It's okay. Alex is better than I thought he'd be."

"That was pretty cool when you took him out like

that," she laughed.

"Caught him off guard, I guess," I chuckled. "It's key to pay close attention to the details. He thought I'd forgotten about my challenge."

"How could you tell?"

"He just wasn't tense."

"Huh, good to know," she sipped her water.

"Hey can I ask you something?"

"Seriously?" She laughed.

"What?"

"Rose, you wouldn't ask me for permission before you read my diary," she had a point. Blair and I never kept secrets. "Fire away."

"Do you like Oliver? And before you answer, I

already know you do."

"I guess."

"C'mon Blair!"

"Is it that obvious?"

"Yeah! And he likes you too, so maybe being here is beneficial for you," I teased.

"He doesn't like me. Besides, even if he did, we couldn't be a thing. We're only here for two weeks, remember?"

I could tell she was sad. Blair had never had the time for anything fun. Even now, this mission is in her way of being a normal teenager when she could've stayed in NYC and lived a normal life, instead of being dragged here. I feel awful for her.

"Hey," I changed the subject, "I learned a new

trick."

"Oh really?"

"Yes, and it'll blow your mind."

"Okay, let's see what you got."

"Brace yourself," I joked. A few years ago, we were at tea with Grandma and Grandpa. When Lewis came to refill our cups, Mia dropped her napkin. Lewis grabbed another from his apron and folded it into a tiny castle. Mia was fascinated. He showed her how to make one and I watched intently. To this day I can still make a napkin castle. All of my childhood memories are so random and vivid, I never really knew why.

"A napkin?"

"Oh you just wait," I chuckled. I folded the napkin into the same tiny castle that Lewis made.

"Wait, how did you do that?"

"I have a secret power."

"Oh, I see. That makes so much sense," we both laughed. About five minutes later, Oliver came out with our food.

"Here you go," he handed us the full plates. "Hey, cool castle!"

"Why, thank you!"

"My older brother made the biggest house of cards once, but I may have destroyed it," he laughed. "I was only three at the time, but he got really mad."

"That sounds like Mia!" Blair laughed at me. "Rose has a little sister named Mia." She turned to Oliver. "Quite the little rascal if you ask me!"

"Do you have any siblings?" he asked Blair.

"No. I'm an only child, but Rose is like a sister to me, and so is Mia, of course. I take care of her while Rose is at work."

"What about school?"

"I go to night school."

"Me, too! We have four schools here on Europa. One elementary school, one middle school, a high school and a college."

"What are the careers you can study for?" I asked.

"I'm not exactly sure. I'm studying robotics, and a friend of mine works in the teleportation facility. I get to visit Headquarters next week for an interview."

"That's fantastic!" Blair said.

"Thanks, I'm excited. Anyway I have to get back

to work now, but I hope you enjoy your meal."

"Thank you," I said. We finished our food and were about to walk out when a message came over the intercom.

"Attention, citizens of Europa," an unfamiliar voice spoke. "This is a crucial announcement. Stop what you are doing immediately. All children sixteen years of age and younger must report to Headquarters by midnight. Parents or guardians seventeen or older must leave their children unaccompanied once they have reached the lobby. SWAT teams will start searching homes at eleven o'clock tonight. All children found remaining in their homes will be taken. This is not optional. This is not a test. Failure to complete this order can and will result in punishment." The message repeated itself and the room went silent.

"Well, that was unexpected," Blair said. I began

typing on my NGT. "What are you doing?"

"Messaging Alex. I have to cancel the afternoon training."

"Why?"

"We're going to Headquarters."

XIX

"Hey, as smart as you are, I don't think this is a good idea," Blair didn't get up.

"Why not?"

"Well, the rule doesn't apply to us. They'll be checking ID cards for age at the front of the building. We're too old to go in. Besides, this is our first day in training, it would be rude to cancel, and Peterson would be furious."

"They're not going to close all of Headquarters for this. Nothing will be shut down, the teleportation facilities will just be busier," I paid for the meal.

"How do you know?"

"Are you kidding me? This place runs on what happens inside of that building."

"Okay, good point. But even if we can get in,

they won't let us into the teleportation facility. Our cards can't open the doors."

"We'll tell whoever is at the doors that it's for the mission. We can say it's for technology studies."

"You're crazy."

"I know, and so are you, which is why you'll agree to come with me," I smiled.

"Fine, but if we get in trouble, it was your idea, got it?"

"Got it," we grabbed our bags and walked to the doors.

"Thanks again!" Blair called to Oliver.

"Oh, wait!" He rushed over, "This is for you," he handed her a small box. "Well, both of you."

"Thanks! You didn't have to," she smiled.

"Don't worry, it's on the house."

"See you later?"

"Sounds great."

"Bye!" I said. We got on our Cycles and drove to Headquarters. The parking garage was full. We spent about half an hour just driving around the building and garage, but found nowhere to park. Looks like everyone was following orders.

"Well, what do we do now?" Blair asked.

"I have a plan."

"Is it a good one?"

"I have a plan."

"So we're going to die," she joked.

"Are you insulting my plan-making skills?" I said

sarcastically.

"Yes, actually. Last time you 'had a plan' we did, in fact almost die."

"We *almost* died." I pointed out. "Now follow me."

"All right," she got back on her Cycle and we drove around the building. The whole city was full of fake plants, and Headquarters had a shrub wall around it. It was about nine feet tall and sat around six feet from the building. Perfect. I pulled over.

"Wait," Blair looked at me. "Okay I'm out."

"No! This is the best part."

"How do you expect us to get back there?"

"I'll hoist you up and toss the Cycles over. You catch them and then I'll help you get back."

"Are you kidding me? You can't just throw a motorcycle fifteen feet in the air. Did you actually think this through?"

"Yeah. See that lamppost over there?" About twenty feet from us stood a huge streetlight. "I can climb up."

"With both Cycles, and an injured hand?" She didn't take me seriously.

"Okay, I have a new plan."

"This better be good."

"I'll climb up and you toss a Cycle to me. I'll throw it on top of the shrub so it won't get damaged. We can do the same with the other one, and then you can climb over. I'll shake the shrub so the Cycles fall down and you catch them. One at a time, of course."

"Do you know how heavy these probably are?"

"I'm pretty sure they're actually light. Because of the minimal design."

"Let's see," she picked one up. "Not bad actually. This might work."

"Hurry, then!" I climbed above twelve feet up the pole.

"Are you sure about this?"

"Yeah just hurry!"

"Okay!" She grabbed one of the Cycles and threw it up to me. I barely caught the wheel with my burned hand. It almost broke the scab, but thankfully didn't. I tossed the second Cycle onto the shrub and slid down.

"What's wrong?" Blair said, pushing over the other Cycle.

"Security cameras. They're everywhere."

"Of course they are."

"We're busted!"

"Nah, were famous. If we can't find a parking spot, we'll make one. Our independence and productivity will impress people."

"Wow. And you thought I was crazy."

"Oh whatever. Now hurry up."

"I'm trying," I can just see the headlines. 'Agents Rose Walters and Blair Davis climb fake plants for fun!' We helped each other over the hedge and pulled the Cycles down. We decided to leave them where they were and walk around the building and into the parking garage. Then we would head inside. It wasn't as easy as it looked, though. Crossing the busy street was awful. On the bright side, I haven't seen any cameras flashing. Not yet at least.

"All right. Let's go to the teleportation facility," I said, casually walking over to an elevator.

"Top floor."

"Thanks," I pushed the button for the highest floor and we shot up. I walked out and down a hallway to the main lobby, leaving Blair. Maybe I didn't think this through. The lobby was packed shoulder to shoulder with kids. I tried to squeeze my way through but found it nearly impossible.

"Ridiculous," I thought to myself, "I can't believe Peterson expects this done by midnight."

"Which country do you want targeted first?" I overheard a conversation from a room marked for 'D2' employees only. I continued eavesdropping.

"Go with North and South America for the first

wave next week," It was Peterson.

"Hospitals first?"

"Yes," he sounded proud.

"Hey," Blair caught up to me, "Why'd you stop?"

"Oh, just waiting for you," I lied. I already felt bad but I needed her for something else. "Hey, you go check out the facility. I'll cause a distraction."

"Got it," she proceeded to the facility doors. I threw my hair into a bun and messaged Blair's NGT on silent mode telling her I'd be with the Cycles. Then I made my way to the elevator door and pressed the button. Once the doors opened, I walked in and pushed the parking garage button. Thankfully nobody else was in there. Just before the doors closed on me, I yelled as frantically as I could. "Bomb!"

XX

The crowd went crazy. I feel bad doing that to kids before they're shipped to Earth without even knowing. But I needed the guard to be distracted so that Blair could slip by. I hope she got the memo and didn't freak out, too. I ran behind the hedge and propped up both Cycles. It took almost half an hour before Blair showed up. She looked worried.

"What happened? What's wrong?" I asked.

"I have bad news. Really bad."

"Did we get caught?"

"No."

"Okay, then what happened?"

"You know Allison? Well she has a daughter."

"How old?" This was horrible news.

"About twelve. I didn't catch her name but she looks just like Allison."

"And?"

"Well, you know how your apartment is still under your parents' names? She's being sent there."

"What?" I yelled.

"Quiet. Allison asked Peterson specifically if she could be sent there because she thought your parents had taken great care of you. She assumed they'd do the same for her daughter."

"Wouldn't Peterson have told her I was alone? I mean of course he knew," I was astonished.

"Look, I don't know the details. But I do know that she's going at ten o'clock."

"This is awful! Who's going to take care of her?

We can't contact anyone from here."

"I'm not sure."

"We need to get out of here. Let's go." We climbed back over the hedge with a few more complications than before, but we eventually made it home. It was only five o'clock. We took a break and talked for a while.

"We should really get some groceries," Blair said. We were both trying to get our minds off of everything we just saw.

"Sure. We've got time to kill."

"I'll go change real quick."

"I'll be in the garage," I rode the elevator downstairs. I've started to wear my oxygen mask in the garage just in case of emergency. I got on my Cycle and started to mess around with my NGT. I looked over to the door waiting for Blair, but her Cycle caught my eye. The box Oliver had given her was still in the back with a slip of paper in the lid. It was clearly addressed to me.

The box itself had 'Davis' written on the top, but the note said 'R.E.W.', my initials, in the now recognizable typed lettering. Another mysterious note. I pulled it out from the crack and unfolded it. 'You need him.' the note read. Strange. Who is 'him'?

"Sorry I took so long," Blair came down, fastening her mask.

"It's fine. Hey, I hate to be a snoop, but there was a note with my initials in your box from Oliver. It's the same one we have been getting, except a different message.

"Let me see," she grabbed it and looked it over carefully. "I think I know who's been leaving them," she whispered as quietly as she could without looking up.

"Who?" I whispered back. I was expecting her to say Oliver, the most reasonable suspect.

"Her," she indicated behind me. At the exit doors of the garage was a girl staring our way. She had a long straight purple ponytail with blue highlights, and wore a heavy amount of edgy makeup. She wore a neon pink, strangely geometric dress, too. Once she saw Blair, she started her bubble-like car and sped away. Blair and I had the same idea to follow her. We immediately got on our Cycles and drove out. The best and worst thing happened as we turned onto the street. Rush hour. We had enough time to make out her vehicle turning right, but we were at a dead stop.

I knew what I was about to do was dangerous, but I had no choice. I turned onto the sidewalk beside us and sped up. I weaved through several pedestrians but nobody was hurt. I turned right on the same street and found myself in the middle of a massive shopping center. Great, she could be anywhere. I parked in an alleyway and covered my Cycle with an old tarp. I took my hair back down so I'd hopefully look somewhat different.

When I rounded the corner, I started to have second thoughts on the girl's odd style. Everyone was wearing it. Almost everyone in sight had neon colored hair and a bright dramatic outfit. Women wore almost vertical iridescent heels, and men dressed in sleek neon patterned suits. I guess I've really never payed attention to the typical citizens of Europa. Oliver was always wearing his uniform, and the people working in Headquarters were always dressed in suits or lab coats.

"Dang," I said to myself, shaking my head. I walked into the first store, assuming she'd hide as soon as she could.

"Oh my!" A woman with a face full of makeup and an exotic dress ran up to me; a crowd of stylists following her. "I can't believe my eyes! Rohana Walters! Here for a makeover!"

"Actually," I tried to explain, but before knew it I was in a salon chair, my hair soaking in a tub of sweet rose water, and my nails and toes were being tended to. There's nothing I can do about my situation now. I tried to look around me without lifting my head from the woman washing my hair, and caught a glimpse of the girl with the purple hair. Someone hidden behind a beam gave her a stack of cash. I was going to say something, but before I could even open my mouth, my face was covered in cleansing water and a mask was applied.

I have to admit that other than my anxiety over the notes and the strange girl, this was actually pretty nice. It's not like I could get up and leave at this point.

"No need for those long locks," a man in green told a lady next to him. She carried a case with all kinds of hair supplies.

"Wait!" I said. "You can't cut my hair!"

"Oh darling," the man spoke, "long hair is so dated! Besides, you have horrid ends," he looked disapproving.

He was right, too. I haven't had my hair cut in almost a year. I just don't have the time.

"Fine, but no more than an inch," I finally agreed. I would love to have short hair, but Mia likes to play with it. She would be so disappointed if I came back with it all chopped off.

"And what color?" The woman asked.

"No color, thank you," she pulled my head out of the tub and toweled it dry. Then she cut off about two inches. I expected as much. My nails and toes were painted and dried, and my hair was slicked to my head with a glittery gel and put into a sleek high ponytail. Straight as could be. My makeup was done simply with only a silver accent in my eyeliner. Beautiful. I left and thanked the stylists, didn't pay a dime. I would have, but they refused.

I opened up the doors on my way out and fastened my mask, my eyes fixed on my NGT. When I looked up I came to the realization that I was the center of attention. Now the cameras had arrived, and I had no clue where Blair was.

XXI

"Walters!" A reporter rushed up to me, "Is it true that you bailed on training to go to the spa?"

"What about Davis? Is she still at the Training Center?"

"Can you give us any insight on the mission?"

"Is Price a good trainer?"

"How far have you gotten in your exercises?"

"I... uh," I tried to come up with a good reason for being here. I didn't want to look like I bailed on Alex to break into Headquarters, cause a riot, and go to the spa. Which, technically I did, except for the spa part.

"Is something going on that you can't tell us?" The questions kept piling on. My ears were ringing and my eyes burned. The flashing cameras, yelling people, and microphones shoved in my face were overwhelming.

I looked for some way to escape and noticed the girl with the purple hair staring at me from an alley across the street.

"Hey look!" I yelled. "It's Blair! Right over there!" The entire crew ran away. I bolted across the street towards the girl. It was a dead end, but she was gone. There were no doors around. I decided to give up. I ran behind a giant trashcan and called Blair.

She picked up right away. "Where are you?"

"Long story. Meet me at home, and stay hidden!"

"Great, what did you do now?"

"Just hurry."

I hung up and took a back road home. I don't think I was spotted. I ran upstairs and locked myself in the penthouse. It wasn't long before Blair showed up.

"Whoa. What happened to you?"

"It's a long story," I laughed.

"But seriously. You've never been that good at eyebrows," she quipped.

"I was attacked by a day spa."

"Sounds cool."

"Aren't you mad at me?"

"What should I be mad at you for?"

"I just bailed on you," I shrugged. "I also made you come here with me. Now we're both being forced to poison a potentially innocent President for reasons we don't even know."

"Rose, you're right. I have every reason to be mad at you," she said, "but I'm not. Sure, maybe you did drive away earlier, but you did it to find whoever has been leaving the notes. And you did! Maybe I'm here now, but it's not because you forced me to come. I wanted to. We may not know what's coming, but none of it is your fault. I'm not mad at you, Rose."

"Really?"

"Yes, really!"

"Thanks for being here for me, Blair," I hugged her.

"Now, you should probably go change."

"Agreed," I walked up the stairs. When I entered my room, the television caught my attention. I don't remember even turning it on, but it looked important. I sat on the bed. It was Allison! She was standing outside of the teleportation facility surrounded by guards and caution tape.

"The whole place was complete chaos," she

spoke. What was complete chaos? I looked closely at the headlines. There was a real bombing at Headquarters! Right after I ran away.

"And what conditions are the facility in?" a reporter asked.

"Well, thankfully, someone in the crowd actually called out a warning of a bomb," she said. "We immediately rushed everyone out of the Capsule Room and shut the doors. We closed the Capsules, too. Thankfully, because we were warned, we had time to seal the Capsules. We weren't exactly sure where the bomb would go off, but the Capsules would be the most logical targets. And we were right," she let out a long sigh. "Thanks to our advanced technology, the bullet and blast-proof doors and walls are in perfect condition, as well as all three Capsules,"

The crowd behind her broke into applause.

"Do you have any idea who the person who warned you was?"

"We will definitely be checking cameras soon. Not only to find our hero, but also whoever planted the bomb."

"And what about the children? Will you still be carrying on with the assignment?"

"Absolutely. We've done a thorough search, and everything seems safe. The order will proceed."

"Well, thank you, Mrs. Dalton! We hope to see you again soon for some more information," the reporter concluded. The screen turned off automatically.

"Wow," I thought to myself. I couldn't decide if I should call myself a hero or villain. I saved the children, and the teleportation facility, but also Peterson's plan. This is awful. What have I done? Someone tried to hurt these kids! But who?

"Rose!" Blair called. "You coming?"

"Yeah," I yelled back, "just a second," I quickly put a shirt over my suit and darted down the stairs and into the garage.

"You good?" Blair asked, fastening her mask.

"Yeah," I got in my Cycle and we drove off. We walked into a grocery store called '7253894' and made a list of things we needed. It was nothing special, mostly fruits and vegetables, white meats, and nuts. Eating healthy would be important over the next two weeks. I was about to leave when Blair's watch went off.

"It's Peterson," she said.

"What does he want now?"

"He wants to know why you canceled on your

first day."

"I'll leave," I said. "You keep shopping."

"No, you've been through enough. I'll go."

"You sure?"

"Yeah," she smiled.

"Thanks," I smiled too.

"See you," she waved goodbye and left.

I grabbed the nearest shopping cart and began reading signs indicating where the groceries were. Obviously this wouldn't be easy. All I saw on the hanging boards were numbers. This was ridiculous! The only real writing I've seen was either on a restaurant menu, an anonymous note, or my watch keyboard! Everything else is numbers.

"What kind of society completely screws up the

average reading system? Not to mention getting rid of the alphabet almost entirely," I complained to myself.

I looked around for an employee. I didn't see anyone official looking, so I walked up to a young boy. He looked about thirteen; I figured he could help me.

"Excuse me," I tapped him on the shoulder.

"Yeah?" He turned around.

"Can you help me find the baking flour? I'm new here and-"

"I know you!" He exclaimed. "You're Rohana Walters!"

"Shhh!" I didn't want to start another riot today. "Yes, that's me," I chuckled.

"Can I get your autograph?" he whispered.

"Sure," I took his pen and wrote my name on a

piece of paper.

"Wow! Thanks," he smiled.

"You're welcome. Now will you please help me find-"

"Have a good day!" he called as he ran off.

"You too," I said. I'll just look for it myself. Process of elimination. I'll walk down each aisle and grab stuff from my list as I go. Perfect! I walked into the aisle closest to me. This wouldn't be easy at all. All of the products were either in a solid white bag or box - marked with a number. I groaned.

"Need some help?" someone said from behind me.

"Yes, actually," I turned around and froze.

XXII

The boy in front of me was wearing the same training suit as I was, except it was white. Peterson told me these were one of a kind, and Alex said nobody else was in training right now. I was really confused.

"You okay?" he asked.

"Oh, yeah I'm fine. Sorry. Do I know you?"

"I don't think so, but I'm pretty sure I recognize you," he smiled.

"I'm pretty sure everyone recognizes me," I chuckled.

"Is it all right if I call you Rohana, then?"

"Just call me Rose," I smiled.

"All right then, Rose, what do you need help with?"

"Well, I can't seem to read anymore."

"What have they been doing to you?" He joked. "Okay, so the alphabet here is different for sure. Every letter has a designated number, and I can't recall them all, honestly. I just moved here a few weeks ago."

"So how do you know what you're looking at?"

"I keep a note in my watch," he pulled up a list of numbers and letters.

"Will you send that to me?"

"Sure, what's your number?"

"Here," I showed him my ID card.

"There you go!" he sent it and my watch buzzed instantly.

"Thanks!"

"Sure thing!"

"Hey, if you don't mind I have a pretty long list. Could you maybe stick around?"

"Absolutely!" he looked surprised. We walked around the store for almost an hour trying to figure out which produce was in what box, what meat went where, and what fruit was good. It was actually pretty fun. By the time seven o'clock came around, I knew Blair would need me.

"Thanks for helping me out! Let me know if I can return the favor," I scanned my last item.

"No problem," he said.

"Hey, I never got your name."

"Oh! It's Cole."

"Cole. I like it!"

"Really?"

"Yeah," I smiled. I really did like the name. And overall I thought he was pretty nice. He was tall, blonde, blue eyes, bright smile, and really helpful.

"Thanks."

"You're welcome. I better be going now, but thanks again!"

"Bye!" he waved as I walked out. I was about to grab my ID card when something occurred to me.

"Cole!" I called.

"What?"

"Keep my number!"

"Oh, uh, sure!" he stuttered. Something about him was different. Good different.

I struggled with trying to fit all of my groceries into the tiny compartment in the back of my Cycle. Once I did, I hurried home. I made my way to the penthouse. Peterson was waiting inside at the table with Blair. He didn't look happy.

"Miss Walters, how many times must I explain that you are expected to follow protocol at all times?" he asked curtly.

"Apparently, not enough," I said.

"Rose, you've disappointed me once again. You had no reason to spy on me and Dalton."

"How did you know we-"?

"I know about everything that goes on here, Rose. You shouldn't have canceled training, either. Especially on your first day."

"I did it to save the facility," I said.

"Which is why I'm here. How did you know there would be an attack?" he asked, raising an eyebrow.

"I can't tell you that."

"Rose," he sighed in frustration, "have you ever wondered why our logo is a honeycomb pattern?"

"I have better things to think about."

"You see," he kept speaking, "everyone here on Europa is like a busy bee. They do as they're told. Every bee has a job. They do it. Every day."

"And?"

"I expect you to work the same way. You will do as you're told without complaints. Understand?"

"Yes."

"And one more thing. When a bee stings, it dies. Don't tell the outside world about your business with us.

Don't sting the public or you personally will suffer the consequences."

"Goodbye, Peterson," I opened the door and gestured for him to leave.

"Goodbye, Walters," he left and slammed the door. Blair and I just stared at each other for a second.

"So..." she hesitated.

"Peterson definitely knows everything. Sees everything. Hears everything."

"For sure."

"So what now?"

"I don't know," she sighed. We should probably keep things in order from now on."

"Definitely."

XXIII

It's been ten days since Peterson visited us. We haven't seen him since. We haven't gone out to eat, haven't canceled training, and haven't even talked to anyone but each other and Alex. Training hasn't been nearly as exciting as it was on our second day here. All we do is high intensity workouts, tumbling, or learning new technology skills.

We've eaten the same thing every day, and followed the same schedule. That's it. Nothing fun to worry about here. Other than the fact that Blair is certain that Alex is flirting with me. He's not though. Blair is desperate for me to be in a relationship, but I really could care less.

"Good morning," Blair said as she made the same green kale smoothie and hard-boiled eggs for breakfast. It was actually a pretty good meal, but we were tired of it.

Alex expected us to eat healthy.

"Good morning," I sat down.

"Hear anything from Alex?"

"No," I sighed. "Probably the same old workout, maybe some tumbling if were lucky. I'm pretty sure I've already dropped ten pounds."

"Same here."

"You know, maybe we should've stayed home."

"It's not like there was an option."

"Maybe there was. Maybe we could've fought back, or secretly told our flight attendant we were being kidnapped."

"Maybe."

"This is awful, anyway. I hate it."

"I do, too. But, what are we going to do about it?"

"There's nothing we *can* do about it."

"It's five-thirty," she smiled sadly.

"Yeah, we should go," we rinsed our dishes and left for the Training Center. Again. When we entered the training room, there were no workout mats on the ground, no notebooks, and no Alex.

"What's this all about?" I looked at Blair.

"I don't know. Maybe there wasn't training today," she turned around to leave.

"Wait! This is going to sound ridiculous, but I think it's a test."

"Test?"

"Yeah. We're going to be out in the field alone

soon. We have to know what to do."

"Well, what are we supposed to get done here?"

"I don't know. Let's look around."

"Let me see if he sent me anything first," she opened her watch. "Nope."

"Great," I said sarcastically, "let's go," we went up to the third level. Instead of the thin workout mats, the floor was bare. Not a trace of Alex was in sight.

"This is stupid."

"Maybe you were right. We should just go," we went back downstairs. We were about to unlock the giant doors when I noticed something. A note. Not like the ones that we'd been getting anonymously, Alex handwrote it. I grabbed it and took it off of the door. Suddenly, alarms went off.

"Wow. This is sure exciting," Blair rolled her eyes.

"What did we do now?" I asked.

"I don't know. Read it."

"It says 'good luck finding your way out. There are ten alarms hidden around the center. For every one you trigger, it's another minute added to your plank tomorrow.' Great."

"We might as well hurry up, then," Blair tried scanning her card. An alarm went off.

"Thanks," I said, rolling my eyes. "Let's check the windows."

"I'll go upstairs," she walked into the elevator.

"Sounds good," I looked around for about half an hour and remembered the compartment I saw behind the weapons shelf. I made my way over to the rack and spotted the compartment with the key in the hole. It also included a note. 'Exit code inside.' Perfect. I knew my lack of patience would pay off. "Hey Blair! Found it!"

"Nice! Wait for me," she came downstairs. "Where is it?"

"There," I pointed behind the weapons.

"What are you waiting for?" she gestured me to grab it. I reached my hand behind the shelf and two alarms went off instantly.

"What?" I jumped.

"I guess they can go off more than once."

"It's a motion sensor. We're trapped."

"Let me try," she reached to turn the key and three alarms went off.

"We can't just sit here when we have the answer right up front of our faces," I reached in and turned the key, then opened the compartment. I read the code and removed my arm. Seven alarms, fourteen minute plank. Hurray.

"No turning back now," Blair punched the code into the pad and the door opened. Alex was standing outside holding a deep red rose.

"Congrats! Wear this to your interview at seven tonight," he gave me the deep red rose. "I'll send you the information later. Go clean up."

XXIV

"Interview?" Blair asked as we left the building.

"Don't ask me," I put my hands up.

"I bet Alex set it up for you."

"What?"

"Oh please. Alex obviously likes you."

"Excuse me? No way."

"Whatever," she teased.

"Mean," I joked. We got on our Cycles and drove home. It was colder than usual. I guess Peterson was right after all. Other than the lack of clouds and dark sky, this climate was much like that in New York. We walked inside and went upstairs and into the penthouse. There was a woman sitting on the couch reading a magazine.

"Who are you?" Blair asked.

"Oh! My apologies," she stood. "My name is Cassandra Violet. I'm the head news reporter here on Europa. Mr. Peterson told me you would be inside, but it seems you were still in the Training Center. I'm so sorry if I scared you."

"No worries," I shook her hand. "I'm Rohana and this is Blair."

"Believe me I know! Everybody does," she shook her head. She was tall, maybe fifty. Her bright blue hair dropped to her shoulders and contrasted her rosy cheeks and pale skin. She seemed nice, other than the other citizens I've encountered so far.

"Nice to meet you, Ms. Violet," Blair shook her hand as well. "Our trainer told us we had an interview before we left today."

"Indeed! I brought a few dresses for each of you to try on, and we'll have our hair and makeup team do you up when we get to the station. All right?"

"Sure," I said. We followed her out to the limo waiting for us. It was identical to Peterson's. Thankfully, he wasn't in there. We got into the backseat and were greeted with food and drinks.

"Mr. Peterson is at the studio helping with set up," she said, pouring a glass of champagne. I mentally rolled my eyes. "Sorry he couldn't be here."

"That's fine," Blair forced a smile.

"Would you like a glass?" she handed me a glass of champagne without hesitation.

"Ma'am, we're seventeen," Blair said.

"So?" she shrugged."

"We're on a diet," I jumped in. "No alcoholic beverages or soda."

"That's just too bad," she took and drank my glass shamelessly.

Blair looked at her with disgust. I suppose I was wrong about Cassandra.

"Oh look! Here already!" We pulled up to a towering skyscraper. It wasn't nearly the size of Headquarters, but it was huge.

"Wow," I looked out the window.

"I know, I know. Hop out!" she rushed us to the doors, obviously in a hurry. We parked on the street outside, but we had no time to put our masks on. By the time we were indoors, Blair and I were panting.

"So," I took a deep breath, "Where to?"

"Floor nineteen for hair, nails, and accessories, twenty-seven for makeup, and twenty-one for outfits. I recommend getting dressed first."

"All right. Thanks," Blair took me by the wrist and darted to the elevator. "Am I the only one who has a bad feeling about her?"

"She's not the only one," I said as we got in.

"What do you mean?"

"The reporters here are rude for sure," I said, remembering my last encounter.

"Oh."

"It's really too bad." We got off on level twenty-one and were practically shoved into dressing rooms.

"Try each one on and tell us what you like best!" a voice called. There were three dresses hanging up. One was a long sleeved light blue maxi dress, one was a knee-length collared maroon dress, and one was a grey cold shoulder dress with a ruffled off the shoulder bodice. I tried each one on but the grey was my favorite. It was light and flowed nicely. It had two layers of different lengths and was slightly shorter than the red one. The torso was fitted, but the skirt had a bell shape and was pretty full. I rarely come across the perfect dress, but I did today.

"Oh my!" A woman in blue covered her dropped jaw when I stepped out. "Stunning!"

She handed me a pair of matching white stilettos.

"So?" Blair stepped out of the dressing room across from me. She was wearing a dark green dress in the same style as the maxi that I tried on. It looked great.

"Wow! You look great!"

"Thanks," she took a matching pair of heels as well.

"Off to makeup!" The woman said, rushing us out the door and into the elevator. When we walked into the studio, the same thing happened. We instantly found ourselves sitting in chairs with our faces being washed and pampered. The man doing my makeup was careful. I found myself wearing deep red lipstick and matching eye shadow.

"That's different," Blair looked over at me.

"Same to you," I gestured to her golden makeup. Before we knew it, we were off again. By the time my hair was done and my accessories were chosen, my nails needed to be fixed. My last surprise manicure had worn off quickly and quite painfully with the intense training and tumbling.

Alex had given me a salve for my burn, which had turned mostly into a giant scab. It still covered my entire palm and most of my fingers. It broke a lot with all of the pressure I had been putting on it from tumbling, especially because I was unable to wear a cloth over it since it was too slippery. It still hurt from time to time, but after my last trip to the salon, I've had only small issues since it was cleaned.

"Can I see your hands please?" a Filipino man with a heavy accent asked.

"Sure," I looked down at my hands and realized that the entire time I had been clutching the rose that Alex gave me. The makeup artist must've noticed it, hence the matching colors. "Excuse me, sir. Can you put this in my hair?" I handed him the rose.

"Buhok na artist, pakiusap!" he yelled something in a different language. A French woman ran over.

"Oui?"

"Nais niya ang rosas sa kanyang buhok.
Pakibilisan," he handed the woman the rose.

"La rose doit d'abord être stérilisée. Un moment,"
she ran off with the rose. I was hoping she wouldn't
dispose of it. The man got started on my nails, which
were done in the same deep red shade. By the time he was
finished, the woman came back with my rose.

"C'est prêt!" she fixed the rose in my bun.

"Salamat," the man nodded and walked off.

"Bien sûr!" she called to him. "You look
beautiful," she bent over my shoulder. "Time to go."

Blair and I were escorted to a room full of lights,
cameras, a table, and five chairs. On our way there, we
actually saw Oliver. His interview that he mentioned last
week just happened to be tonight on a different news

channel. Blair was happy to see him. Cassandra and Peterson were sitting down waiting for us. But who was the fifth chair for?

The set manager called from behind a camera. "We're live in two minutes! Sit down!"

"Where's Price?" Cassandra asked.

"You mean Alex?" I asked.

"Yes, he should be here," Peterson said.

"What?" Blair asked. Just then, the door opened and Alex walked in wearing the same white suit as Peterson wore. He sat down and smiled at me.

"I like it," he gestured to the rose in my hair. "You look beautiful."

Someone then yelled, "And we're live in three, two one!"

XXV

We sat and waited for the set manager to give us the cue. She pointed.

Cassandra spoke, "Welcome back, Europa! Today we have an exclusive interview featuring Rohana Walters and Blair Davis! Tomorrow is their last day on Europa. Their Training Manager, Alexander Price, and the one and only president of our beloved association, George Peterson, accompany them today! We really are so honored to have them here."

"Hello everyone!" Peterson smiled. "I'm sure you all know their names by now, but how about we have our special guests introduce themselves! Rohana? Tell us your story. What do you think of Europa so far?"

"Well, it certainly has been much different than New York! The technology here has really blown me away. I can't wait to finish up training."

"Speaking of training," Cassandra said, "how has that been going for you?"

"It's definitely tough. We've been working on lots of moves and experimenting with technology. Other than that, I can't remember the last day I didn't have to work out," I joked. Everyone began laughing for effect.

"Blair?"

"Oh, it's been really great! I've been having lots of fun. I've never really gotten as much attention as I am now, so it's a bit overwhelming, but overall I'm really enjoying my time here."

"Other than the people in Headquarters, do you enjoy the citizens?"

Blair shook her head, "I haven't really been out much, so I wouldn't know."

"I would have to agree with her. The overall

intelligence here is obvious, though. When I was having my hair and makeup done earlier, a Filipino man was having a conversation with my hair stylist, who was French. They both spoke their native languages, but understood each other perfectly. It was truly amazing and really beautiful to see that happening. I can't wait to support the cause and build the population through this mission," I smiled at Peterson. I wanted to see his reaction to my comment, not forgetting how confident Oliver was when he told us that he thought we'd be testing for IQ. I felt bad for them. They had no idea that we were on a mission to kill.

"That's amazing! We can't wait to see what you have coming for us. Alexander, how has your experience with the girls been so far?"

"Well," he said, "it's been really fun. Of course we have to take training seriously, but, we've been enjoying what we can."

"And what did you think when you first met Blair and Rohana?"

"Well, when I was visiting Earth, I actually met Rohana three times, I think. Of course she didn't know what was going on, and she wasn't too happy with me trying to save her."

"Save her?"

"The reason I was on Earth was due to a planned attack in a location Rohana was supposed to be at that time. Blair was there, too. I'm just glad they made it out safely."

"We are, too! Rohana, what was going though your head at that moment?"

"I actually thought he was stalking me," I laughed. "Now I feel bad for it."

"Me too," Blair said. "I was definitely upset about the whole thing. We weren't told what was going on until we were halfway to Paris."

"Not quite halfway," Peterson smiled at the camera.

"How come?" I knew that now Peterson would have to give us an answer to the question he'd been trying to avoid for the past week.

"Various reasons. I didn't want them running around telling the public that I was a crazed liar. I would be arrested, interrogated, the people would be suspicious for years. Everything would turn into one big conspiracy." He had a point I suppose.

"I understand," Cassandra chuckled.

We talked and discussed the mission, the fake one that is, and a few other things. The interview itself was only an hour, but we didn't get to leave until late. I was exhausted.

"I'm so hungry right now it's not even funny," Blair stuffed her face into a pillow the second we got home.

"We haven't eaten since this morning," I agreed.

"Healthy food is gross though," she whined.

"Too bad. Eat an apple."

"Fine."

"Tomorrow is our last day here, you know."

"You sure you want to do this?"

"No."

"I asked the wrong question. We kind of have to do this. I mean do we really have a choice at this point?"

"Absolutely. And I have a plan."

XXVI

The next morning, I wasn't feeling well. I wasn't sick, but I was scared. You know the feeling when you're about to poison someone? That feeling. Other than the hate for Peterson that I have because of his audacity to do this to us, I'm also upset that today the people of Europa will be cheering us on, oblivious to what the real situation is. I can't stand this. But, ever since I found out about the Strychnine, I've been planning to 'accidentally' mess up. If I can trigger an alarm, getting arrested for being innocent would be better than dealing with the shame of being guilty.

"Blair!" I yelled from my room, wondering if she were already awake.

"What?" she was downstairs.

"Never mind," I walked into the bathroom and did my hair and makeup, put on my suit, and went downstairs. "How did you wake up so early?"

"I didn't sleep."

"What?"

"I'll sleep on the flight. What's your plan?"

"Plan?" I gestured to the security cameras around us. Peterson would be watching us. Especially today.

"For your waving technique?" she was catching on.

"Oh!" I smiled. "Side to side."

"Great," we left without breakfast, and went straight to the Training Center. We didn't have training today, but Alex wanted to meet with us before we left. Once we arrived, the paparazzi were on the move. Most of the press had unlimited access to our locations and conversations today. Every move that we made would be broadcast like a reality television production. We ignored the reporters, questions, and cameras. Once we arrived at the door to the Training Room, Alex opened it right away.

"Sorry fellas," he said to the cameramen as he shut the door, "no entry allowed."

"Hey."

"Hey," he rubbed his hands together nervously. "Follow me," we entered a small dark storage closet.

"What's going on?" Blair asked.

"Listen, I lied to you guys. Strychnine isn't painless. It's awful and-"

"I know," I interrupted.

"I didn't!" Blair said.

"There's no time to explain it. And I'm so sorry."

"You're telling us this now?" Blair shook her head.

"I have a plan. Take this." He handed me an exact replica of the strychnine vials in our bags.

"More strychnine?"

"No. It's an anesthetic powder. It'll be enough to make someone appear dead for six hours, which is enough for you to get home. After he 'resurrects' it'll be Peterson's problem. Got it?"

"Wow. Thank you," I hugged him.

"Alex are you sure you want to do this? You could get in big trouble."

"I'm sure. Now let's go. Smile and wave!" We opened the doors to flashing cameras and invasive interviewers. Once all three of us were in the limo, I felt relieved. Sure, maybe Alex ruined my life for a hot minute, but in a way, I guess he made up for it.

"We're here," the limo driver said as we stopped. People lined the streets. Almost all of them held up signs and banners saying 'thank you' or 'good luck' for us. I was heartbroken, but I smiled anyway. The entire time we've been here, almost everyone has been so excited for us. They all thought we'd be building and supporting UIA. I wonder what they'd all think when they never heard of us again, or when they realized that nobody was tested. Smile and wave, smile and wave. We walked into Headquarters and Peterson and Cassandra greeted us, along with a film crew.

"Cameras rolling in three, two, one!" We all smiled.

"We're back with our favorite girls!" Cassandra exclaimed. "Today they will be sent back to Paris for a lovely overnight stay as a gift for their hard work and dedication," she turned to us. "Surprise!"

"Wow!" Blair exclaimed. "That's amazing!"

"Totally! Thank you all so much!"

"Oh, we're not the ones to thank," she smirked. Blair and I each gave a puzzled expression and looked at Peterson. He shrugged.

"It's Mr. Price."

"Alex?" I said, surprised.

"Well, yeah. One day in training, I overheard you talking to each other about how you wished you could've stayed in Paris for more than just a taxi ride, and I thought you both deserved that." Everyone around us cheered.

"How sweet," Cassandra sighed. "Isn't it folks?" Everyone cheered.

"All right. All right," Peterson shook his head. "We unfortunately have to leave now, wish us luck!" We all waved.

Teleporting back to Earth was not nearly as exciting as arriving. When we arrived at the Paris facility, everyone rushed up so say their goodbyes. Except for Allison. I didn't see her at all today. Once we made our way back through the abandoned museum, we caught a taxi. This was it.

XXVII

We exited the taxi at a nice hotel in the middle of the city. Peterson told us he would be driving back to the station.

"Have fun," he waved and the driver sped away.

"What the heck," I shrugged. "We might as well just enjoy our time here. It might be the last time we get to have some fun."

"I guess so," she said. We went and checked into our hotel room, then headed out to the Eiffel tower. I have only been to Europe once. It was for a school trip when I was a freshman. We went to London. Paris was much different than I expected it to be. The Eiffel tower was amazing, and the food was fantastic. I just wish I'd been able to enjoy it more. Having the stress of the upcoming events on my mind made it hard to have fun.

"This really is nice," Blair said as we made our way back to the hotel room.

"Yeah, I think we should sort out this past month though."

"What do you mean?"

"I don't know, this is so confusing."

"Let's just map it out. Start to finish."

"Okay. Two weeks ago, I woke up thinking it was going to be a normal day. I took Mia to grab some flowers, where I met Alex. Afterwards I went to go and see Grandma. We talked for a while at her house, then went to the local coffee shop on Sixteenth Street where we saw Alex again."

"After that, you saw me at the funeral, I explained what was going on with Alex, and then the services were about to start."

"We sat down, and Alex rushed me over to where he was sitting near the funeral area. I told him to go away, but he warned me of something that was going to happen, he didn't explain what it was though."

"The bombs," Blair continued. "A few nights ago, Alex explained that it was a planned attack, but I didn't say who it had been planned by or why."

"Next thing we know, bombs go off. We go to your mom's house, have some lunch, and discuss the recent events."

"Before we know it, Peterson is knocking on our door and forcing us to come with them to Paris. We agree out of fear. On the plane he explains that we are apparently geniuses."

"For the next two weeks we started training for a mission to kill the President, and we don't even know why. We know that Peterson didn't tell anybody the real truth about the mission either."

"Sounds great," We both sighed. This has been pretty crazy so far.

"So what are we going to do? This whole thing is so ridiculous."

"Alex gave us the anesthetic powder."

"You think it will work? I mean, you saw how Peterson has been watching our every move."

"I hope so, but this is our only chance anyway. Would you rather do worse?"

"Good point."

"We should get some sleep," we changed in to the silk pajamas that had been given us to our on our flight to Paris two weeks ago. I stood at our window looking out at the city for a while. It wasn't quite as magnificent as Europa, but I'd rather be here than that miserable place. As great of an experience we had up there, the reason we were there was horrible and I'll never forget it. I just hope that this is over quickly.

XXVIII

The next morning, we had to rise early for our flight to New York. Blair and I hardly spoke until we were on the plane.

"Ella?" I asked. Ella, the attendant who had helped us on our flight to Paris, showed up carrying a tray of tea.

"Girls!" she gasped. "How was your time in Paris?"

"Great!" Blair nodded.

"Sorry I didn't see you sooner, I was working in coach."

"What brings you up here?"

"Actually, a fellow passenger asked me to give this to you," she slipped me a small piece of paper. I didn't need to read it to know exactly what it was.

Another note. Whoever has been giving these to us is on the flight right now. I quickly stuffed it into my pocket.

"Thanks, Ella."

"No problem!" she walked off.

"What the heck?" Blair asked.

"This is unsettling."

"No kidding."

"What now?" I whispered. Peterson was back on Europa, but we had to keep it on the down low just in case.

"There's nothing we can do."

"Ladies and gentlemen," the intercom turned on, "this is your pilot speaking. We hope you enjoyed your flight to New York City! Please fasten your seatbelts, as we will be landing shortly." Once the announcement was over, we gathered our things and made our descent. The trip through the airport was busy, and we caught a cab to my apartment. Peterson gave us our next flight information last night before he left.

"So, how are we supposed to explain all of this?" I asked as we entered my empty apartment.

"I'm not sure. They don't remember us leaving."

"What about Mia?"

"I don't know, let's just get there as soon as we can."

"Good idea." We walked inside, left our bags and changed clothes. I hid our suits so that we wouldn't have to explain what they were. We'd still have to wear them for the mission. Once we were finished up, we got in my car and drove to Grandma's. The gates were open, so I drove right in. Everything looked the same as we approached the door. I hesitated to knock.

Blair looked at me, "Well? What are you waiting for?"

"I just hope they're not mad."

"They won't be."

"All right, if you say so. Here goes nothing," I knocked. What happened next threw everything off. Someone I didn't recognize, a little girl about Mia's age, answered the door.

"Hello?" she asked. "How can I help you?"

I tried to sound like I wasn't confused. "Oh, hi. Does Mrs. Walters still live here?"

"Absolutely! And can I ask for your names please?"

"Rose and Blair."

"Rose? You mean Mia's older sister?"

"Yes."

"Wow! I can't wait to tell Grandma!" her face lit up. "Just a minute," she darted away.

"Well," Blair looked at me, "that was unexpected. Do you know her?"

"No. She could be in Mia's class. Could she?"

"Maybe."

"These past few weeks have just been getting weirder and weirder."

"Tell me about it." We waited a minute or two. Finally, the door opened again. Before I could say anything, Grandma wrapped her arms around me.

"Grandma I-"

"Don't worry about it. We know."

"You know? About what?"

"Follow me. Blair, sweetheart, your mother is in the living room."

"Thank you, Grams."

"Where are we going?"

"Your Grandfather's study," she led me up the staircase and handed me a small slip of paper. The same shape and size as the notes we'd been getting for the past two weeks. The same typewriter font. I nearly screamed. "Charles gave me this before he left for Paris."

I unfolded the paper. 'Don't worry about Rose. We have this under control. If she returns safely, don't ask questions.' The black ink pierced my eyes. Could all of the notes have been from him? No. He's gone. That would be impossible. Wouldn't it?

"Wow. Okay."

"I won't ask you questions, Rose. I'm just glad you're back safely."

"Who's the girl?"

"Her name is Antalya. About a week after you left, I went to your apartment to get Mia's clothes and things. She was sitting inside by herself."

"Why?"

"Didn't you hear? Apparently in Paris, there are too many orphans. The adoption rates have gone down too far. Nobody is allowed to have children until they're all gone. Major cities all over the globe have had children sent to each home with a married couple with both spouses under the age of forty.

"I'm seventeen and live alone."

"Your apartment is still under your parents' names."

Then it hit me. Antalya is Allison's daughter. The children in Paris were the children sent to Earth from Europa. What was going on? I fell silent.

"Rose? Are you okay?"

"Yeah. I just zoned out there. Sorry."

"I know, it's a lot to take in."

"Listen, I need to go," I checked my watch our flight was in three hours. "I'll be back in two days. No questions asked. Right?"

"I'm trusting you, Rose."

"Thank you," I ran downstairs. "Blair! It's time to go!" before I knew it we were both in the car.

"What's wrong?" she asked.

232

"I'll explain everything on the plane."

"If you say so. But hurry."

"I know."

XXIX

"Ladies and gentlemen, this is your pilot speaking. We will now be taking off. Please, buckle your seatbelts and focus your attention to the front of the plane, as our flight attendants will be giving basic flight emergency information and instructions. Enjoy your flight to the beautiful Washington, D.C." We sat down and Blair looked at me, obviously wanting answers.

"Antalya. That's the little girls name."

"So?"

"Grandma found her at my apartment. She's Allison's daughter."

"What?" Blair almost yelled. The flight attendant giving safety protocol scowled. "Sorry," she whispered.

"You were right about my apartment. That's exactly where she was sent."

"Why though?"

"There is a new law stating that nobody is allowed to have kids because there are too many orphans in Paris."

"The kids from Europa."

"Exactly. They're being sent to homes here."

"How come? They have space on Europa."

"I don't know. Things aren't adding up."

"Things never add up."

"What are we even doing? Breaking into the White House, faking a murder?"

"Alex said he'd get us in. We won't land until midnight. Our suits will keep us hidden in the dark."

"Oh crap!"

"What?"

"I left the suits in the car!"

"No, I grabbed them."

"You're a lifesaver, Blair."

"I know. Let's get some rest. When it's time to land we'll figure this out."

"Okay." I fell asleep almost right away. By the time we were off the plane, the situation really hit me. I got on my watch right away and connected our earpieces, then called Alex.

"Hello?" he picked up immediately.

"Hey. We're at the airport.

"I want you to go on mute then ask for a cab to the Washington monument. Get back online when you're there."

"Got it," I turned it off. Because we didn't have any bags, we made it out quickly and got a cab.

"Washington monument please," I asked and handed the driver some cash.

"At midnight?" he scoffed.

"Yes," Blair snipped, "at midnight. Are you going to do your job or not?"

"Slow down, princess. We're on our way."

"Thank you." We made our way into the glowing city and stopped by the towering structure. We got out without a word and got back on the line with Alex.

"Okay, now start walking to the White House."

"Walking?" I almost yelled. "I can't even see it from here."

"Relax. Its barely even a mile."

"Again, this is going to take seven years," Blair shook her head.

"We'd better hurry up, then," I started down the sidewalk. Once we made it there, I got back online again.

"Were here, and we've already jumped both fences."

"Okay. Go to the left side. I've got the guards distracted and the cameras are off."

"Got it," we ran over.

"Are your suits on?"

"They're under our clothes."

"Change out and jump the fence into the garden."

"Okay," we quickly changed and helped each other over the fence. "We're in."

"Go though the back door. It's unlocked."

"How did you do that?"

"Go!"

"Fine!" We ran in. It was beautiful! The halls were lined with golden wallpaper and chandeliers twinkled in the moonlight beaming through the large windows.

"Okay. This is where it gets tricky. The cameras are disabled, but the lasers aren't. Can you do the tumbling routine we worked on?"

"You sound like a cheerleader."

"Shut up," he laughed. "Do you see the tiny black boxes on the left wall?"

"Yeah."

"Each one has a laser pointed straight across to the

other wall. Tumble over them. Quietly!

"Yeah, yeah. Whatever. Let's go." We made it to the back wall without triggering any alarms."

"Nice. Now, up the stairs and into the eighth door on the right. There's a laundry room. Go in there."

"Why?"

"Just trust him," I heard Peterson on another line.

"When did you get here?"

"I'm outside the White House as of thirty seconds ago. Hurry up."

"Okay," we ran upstairs and into the laundry room.

"There's a laundry shoot on the back wall. It leads to the President's room."

"Does it have a ladder or something?"

"No. You're going to have to scoot your way up. Have fun."

"Thanks a lot." It took us a while to make it up, but we did. We crawled out and into a small room.

"That's it. I'm out, this is all you now."

"Bye, I muted the earpiece.

"Let's go," Blair nodded.

"You sure?"

"Yeah. Well just pour the anesthesia that Alex gave us into his drink and that's it. We're out."

"Okay," I opened the door to the main bedroom and almost screamed. President Voltaire was sitting on the edge of his bed, wide awake.

"Hello girls," he smiled. "I've been expecting you."

XXX

I stood in silence.

"Come. Have a seat," he gestured to a small table with a tray of tea and sugar.

"How did you know we -"

"Were coming to kill me?"

"Well, we-"

"I know you didn't mean for any of this."

"Mr. President, we are so sorry."

"Don't be. You were only hoping to be able to return home. I understand that George wouldn't even give you an explanation for all of this."

"You know Peterson?"

"Of course. I'm a part of UIA. He's my boss. Not

the brightest person. Now, wouldn't you like to know why you're here to dispose of me?"

"I suppose," I said shyly.

"Sit down then, I won't bite."

"Thank you," Blair took a seat.

"So, as you know everyone that works in the government is a member of UIA, yes?"

"Yes."

"And you know that the children have been sent down here."

"Yes."

"Do you know about the hospitals?"

"No. What about them?"

"They've been shut down. Just like NASA."

"What do you mean?"

"The reason that has been given to the public states that NASA went bankrupt going to Mars, and that the hospitals have suffered the same by spending their money on cancer studies."

"Patients can't live without the hospitals!" Blair said.

"Exactly."

"They want people dying?" I asked.

"Peterson believes that the sick don't matter. They can't contribute to society."

"That's awful!"

"Indeed. Now do you know why all of the children are being sent down?"

"Something about Europa's air conditions being

unhealthy, right?"

"No. The people on Europa will continue to have children. After each child is born, they are given immunity vaccinations. They'll be perfect beings. Every ten years, they're sent here! What will happen if the ordinary people can no longer have children?"

"The immune, smart, and healthy children will become the future generations," I almost whispered.

"And as for the hospitals? Well, disposing of the sick will simply speed up the process."

"This was all Peterson's idea?"

"Yes."

"What a monster," Blair sighed.

"It's smart," I said. "It's awfully horribly smart. How can we stop this?"

"That's where you come in."

"Us? I thought we were done here."

"We have a plan to stop all of this."

"We?"

"The Universal Defense Association. Or UDA for short. We're based on Callisto."

"There's another organization just like UIA?"

"Absolutely. Except we're much more advanced, twice as large as UIA, and our teams are stronger. We're not afraid of anything up there, and from what my son has told me, neither are you."

"I didn't know you had a son!" Blair exclaimed.

"His name is Cole. It's a long story, but he's on Callisto now. I understand you've met him."

"Yeah, I did. This is crazy."

"Rose, does your Grandmother know about any of this?" Voltaire asked.

"No, why? Should I tell her?"

"No. The bombing at the funeral was staged by Peterson to kill her. For the same reason you're here to kill me. I'm the only other person he thinks could know of his plans. He thought your Grandpa may have told her, too. Therefore making her just as much of a threat as I am."

"My Grandpa?" The room went silent.

"Rose," he smiled, "your Grandfather is the president of UDA. He's alive. He left because Peterson's plan was going into effect. He faked his death."

"What the heck," I covered my mouth. Grandpa is alive! I knew it! He went to Paris to use the teleportation facility!

"We haven't got much time. You need to go."

"What about you?"

"My time here is up," he stood and walked over to his nightstand.

"What are you doing?"

"Your convenient strychnine substitute wasn't a bad idea, but if Peterson finds out I leaked this information, he'll use me to stop you. I'm now a threat. He was right, people don't like bees who sting."

"What? You can't kill yourself!"

"I have no other choice," he took a tube of white powder from his drawer and poured it into his tea.

"Please! You can make it out!"

"Go, get out of here as soon as you can. Cole is outside waiting by the monument. He'll explain what comes next. Cheers," he took one small sip and that was it.

Blair took my arm and we ran out of the room. We reached the giant front doors and threw them open. Peterson was outside, accompanied by a squad of bodyguards surrounding us.

"Oh, girls," he stepped forward. "What a shame. I really thought I could trust you."

"What are you talking about?"

"Please. Do you really think I'm stupid? Next time, I'd think twice when you mute the wrong end of the line. Get in the car. Now."

About The Author

I've never had to write any sort of formal autobiography before, and there was no way I was going to write this in third person, so here we are. Obviously, this is not a completely professional or very serious book. I only wrote this at twelve years old, and had it published by thirteen. In no way did I intend for this to have a deep hidden meaning, or dramatic purpose, it was simply fun for me to do. This is my first novel, but it definitely will not be the last. Once I finish this trilogy, I plan on writing several things that are definitely more serious. Over the months between finishing and publishing this novel, I began to realize and learn more about the people and the planet. I would love to write a couple of books that raise awareness about both. I'm not sure how to close this, either. I really do hope that my writing career continues to grow, all with the help of my readers. Again, you've given me amazing opportunity by choosing this book, I hope you found it exciting and enjoyed it just as much as I did.